跟著阿滴滴妹

說出溜英文

網路人氣影片系列

《10句常用英文》大補帖

英語教學 YouTuber

阿滴 & 滴妹 / 著

哈囉我是阿滴！不知不覺這個開頭介紹已經用三年了。在累積這麼多的網路教學內容之後，這是第二次透過出版品跟大家分享我對英文學習的熱情！

我對於英文教學的理念一直都是「要喜歡英文，才能學好英文」。因此，我對節目設計的目標，就是要增加趣味性和可看性，讓觀眾願意點進來並耐心看完整部影片。畢竟大家都是在下班下課後，才有時間看影片，很多人單純只想看娛樂性的內容。除了研究如何充實教學內容外，我也在主題切入點跟包裝方式下了很多功夫。我相信，當知識性的節目有足夠的娛樂性時，就會受到觀眾喜歡！過去三年來，阿滴英文證實了這一點。我們的頻道擁有 150 萬個訂閱者，是全台灣第一名的知識型頻道，教學節目在網路上也都可以達到幾十萬的觀看次數，讓很多人重拾對英文學習的興趣。

我在這裡要談談當初設立頻道的初衷。我在 2016 年下定決心辭職成為全職 YouTuber 時，頻道經歷了一段低潮期。當時的我想要製作更專精、更具有深度的內容，所以開發了許多新的教學節目，特別探討文法及語言學。不過，在嘗試三個月之後，觀眾反而越來越少，頻道的其他影片也乏人問津。那時我才真正體會到：一個單純「在 YouTube 上教英文」的頻道是無法成功的。生硬的知識要靠正確的包裝方式，才能夠被更廣大的觀眾接受。

在這不長也不短的三個月裡，我們持續設計各種節目，從失敗中學習，慢慢抓到觀眾的胃口。最後，我們終於創造了一個成功的節目模式，也就是第一集的《10 個常用的英文句子》。這個節目也許不是現在頻道上點閱率最高的，但絕對是我跟滴妹心目中最有意義的系列。不光是因為它是我們經過三個月的 trial and error 好不容易找到的成功配方，更是因為它代表了整個頻道的設計理念：有趣、實用、生活化。

這本書同樣秉持著這三個設計理念，把《10 個常用的英文句子》系列的精神完全貫徹其中，內容也加以延伸，匯集成更上一層樓的英語會話教材。本書內容包含六大生活情境「食衣住行育樂」，再細分為 66 個實用的對話主題，讓你碰到生活中的各種大小事，都可以輕鬆用英文應對。更重要的是，整本書的內容設計相當有趣，例句絕對可以讓你會心一笑！

如果你是固定收看我們網路節目的小滴，相信你對這種趣味學習的內容一定不陌生！在這本書裡，你會更扎實地學習到很多英文會話的重點。如果你是單純對英文會話有興趣的讀者，希望你可以用輕鬆的心態翻閱這本書，讓每一段有趣的對話加深你對各種情境的印象，並且在需要的時候讓英文成為你的超能力，勇敢地把英文秀出來！

阿滴

Contents

食
012

衣

048

住
078

行
098

GLOBAL TAX FREE

育

132

樂
166

Ray
覺得自己是主角，
負責問奇怪的問題
跟迷路。

Crown
實際上的主角，
愛吃、愛睡覺，
但其實很精明。

Jane
會按照對話需求
改變角色設定的
奇女子。

Joe
來自舊金山，
基本上是一位
損友。

掃描音檔

QR Code:

這本書每頁都有錄製音檔，只要用手機
掃描 QR Code 就可以聽到阿滴滴妹親自
示範單字、例句、對話給你聽！若想下
載全書音檔，版權頁也有提供連結。另
外補充的影片也會用 QR Code 呈現，讓
你能搭配影音閱讀！

本書使用說明

主題：
全書分成「食衣住行育樂」
6 大主題，主題之下有 7-13
則主題對話。

暖身活動：
以「阿滴英文」頻道
上《10 句常用英文》
的相關影片內容作為
暖身開場，並將 10 個
句子列出，大家可以
邊看影片、邊讀句子
更清楚喔！

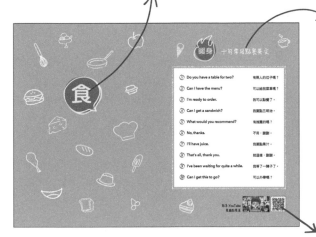

影片 QR Code：
直接拿起手機掃描
QR Code，就能看到
阿滴影片的 10 句常
用英文。

單字片語：
每篇對話先介紹重要的單字與片
語，並提供一則例句，先熟悉單
字片語之後再進入對話。

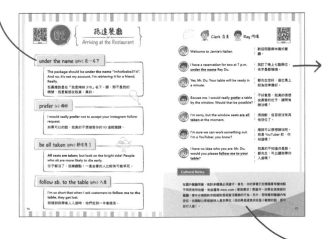

對話：
66 則生活主題對話，
有梗又充實的內容讓
你快樂學英文！

延伸補充：
補充相關文化或語言
知識，或是延伸的學
習影片，讓你英文學
習不間斷！

暖身　十句常用點餐英文

①	Do you have a table for two?	有兩人的位子嗎？
②	Can I have the menu?	可以給我菜單嗎？
③	I'm ready to order.	我可以點餐了。
④	Can I get a sandwich?	我要點三明治。
⑤	What would you recommend?	有推薦的嗎？
⑥	No, thanks.	不用，謝謝。
⑦	I'll have juice.	我要點果汁。
⑧	That's all, thank you.	就這樣，謝謝。
⑨	I've been waiting for quite a while.	我等了一陣子了。
⑩	Can I get this to go?	可以外帶嗎？

取自 YouTube
餐廳點餐篇

餐廳訂位
Making a Reservation

make a reservation (phr.) 訂位；預約

Hi, I **made a reservation** about a year ago. Does that count?

我是一年前訂的位，現在還算數嗎？

a table for two (phr.) 兩人桌

I'm alone, but I ask for **a table for two**, so that I feel less lonely.

我很邊緣但是我都訂兩人桌，感覺比較不孤單。

booked up (phr.) 訂位滿了

We're all **booked up**. All those empty tables you see are mere illusions.

我們訂位全滿囉。那些空桌都是假的，是你眼睛業障重。

cancel (v.) 取消

I swear I won't **cancel** our plans this weekend, unless someone better-looking asks me out.

我發誓不會取消我們週末的計畫，除非有更正的人來約我。

Clerk 店員 Ray 阿滴

002

 Jamie's Italian. How may I help you? | 傑米義式餐廳，您好。

 I'd like to **make a reservation**. | 我想要訂位。

 Sure, for which day and at what time? | 沒問題，請問要什麼日期和時間？

 Do you have **a table for two** tonight? Somewhere around 7 p.m.? | 今晚有兩人的位子嗎？大概晚上七點鐘？

 My apologies. I'm afraid we're already **booked up** for the night, but we do have a table for two at 7 p.m. tomorrow. | 不好意思，我們今晚已經客滿了。但明晚上七點有兩人的位子。

 Sure. I'll take it. | 好啊，那我要預訂。

 May I have the name on the reservation and a phone number where we can reach you? | 請問訂位大名和聯絡電話？

 Touche, trying to get my number, are you? | 很會喔，想要到我的電話4不4～

 Or I could always **cancel** your reservation. | 或是我也可以取消您的訂位。

 Just kidding! Let me just give you my number. | 開玩笑的啦～我的電話現在給你齁。

003

抵達餐廳
Arriving at the Restaurant

under the name (phr.) 在…名下

The package should be **under the name** "imhotbabe316".
And no, it's not my account. I'm retrieving it for a friend.
Really.

包裹應該是在「我是辣妹 316」名下。額，那不是我的
帳號，我是幫朋友取貨。真的。

prefer (v.) 偏好

I would really **prefer** not to accept your Instagram follow
request.

如果可以的話，我真的不想接受你的 IG 追蹤邀請。

be all taken (phr.) 都沒有了

All seats **are taken**; but look on the bright side! People
who sit are more likely to die early.

位子都沒了，但樂觀點！一直坐著的人比較有可能早死。

follow sb. to the table (phr.) 入座

I'm so short that when I ask customers to **follow me to the
table**, they get lost.

我矮到我帶客人入座時，他們走到一半會跟丟。

 Clerk 店員 Ray 阿滴

004

 Welcome to Jamie's Italian.

歡迎蒞臨傑米義式餐廳。

 I have a reservation for two at 7 p.m. **under the name** Ray Du.

我訂了晚上七點兩位，名字是都瑞瑞。

 Yes, Mr. Du. Your table will be ready in a minute.

都先生您好，座位馬上就為您準備好。

 Excuse me. I would really **prefer** a table by the window. Would that be possible?

不好意思，我真的很想坐靠窗的位子，請問有辦法嗎？

 I'm sorry, but the window seats **are all taken** at the moment.

很抱歉，但目前沒有其他空位了。

 I'm sure we can work something out. I'm a YouTuber, you know?

應該可以想想辦法吧。我是 YouTuber 欸，你知道嗎？

 I have no idea who you are. Mr. Du, would you please **follow me to your table**?

我真的不知道你是誰。都先生，可以讓我帶你入座嗎？

Cultural Notes

在國外餐廳用餐，有許多禮儀必須遵守。首先，你的穿著打扮應隨著用餐地點不同而有所改變，有些還有 dress code（著裝要求）需遵守。如果是很高級的餐廳，穿牛仔褲跟帆布鞋絕對是相當沒禮貌的行為。另外，即使看到餐廳內有空位，也請耐心等候接待人員來帶位（但如果是速食店或是小餐館的話，即可自行入座）。

005

餐點很慢來
The Order Is Late!

take so long (phr.) 太久

Karma **takes so long**. I need to kick your butt right now.
報應要等太久,我現在就要打爆你。

more than usual (phr.) 比一般多

I broke down three times in the past two minutes, which was a bit **more than usual**.
過去兩分鐘裡,我崩潰了三次,比平常還多一點。

starving (adj.) 飢餓的

I'm **starving**. I need my second breakfast now.
我快餓死了,我要吃第二份早餐。

get back to sb. (phr.) 回覆(某人)

I'll **get back to you** when I get back to you.
我爽回覆你的時候就會回覆你。

Crown 滴妹　 Ray 阿滴　 Waiter 服務生　
006

 What's **taking so long**? We've been waiting for 30 minutes.

他們怎麼這麼慢？我們已經等三十分鐘了耶。

 Yeah, it's taking them **longer than usual.** Perhaps there're just too many customers today.

對啊，動作好像比平常還要慢，可能今天客人比較多吧。

 Maybe we can ask?

我們可以問問看嗎？

(Waiter walks by.)

（店員經過。）

 Excuse me.

不好意思。

 Yes. How may I help you?

有什麼可以為您服務的地方嗎？

 Our order is late. We've been waiting for 3 days already. We're **starving**.

我們的餐點一直沒來。我們已經等了三天，真的快餓死了。

 I just sat you guys down 3 minutes ago. But let me check with the kitchen and I will **get back to you**.

我三分鐘前才帶你們入座。但我會跟廚房問問看狀況，待會跟您說。

Time flies when you're hungry.

肚子餓的時候，時間總是過得特別快。

討論食物好吃
The Food Is Awesome!

crispy (adj.) 脆的

I love **crispy** food so much that I deep-fry my rice.
我超愛吃脆的東西，我連飯都會用炸的。

tender (adj.) 嫩的

This pork chop is so **tender** it can be my pillow.
這塊豬排嫩到可以當我的枕頭了。

juicy (adj.) 多汁的；精彩的

Give me all the sweet, **juicy** details!
讓我聽精彩的細節！

top-notch (adj.) 頂級的

This taxi driver must be **top-notch**. He is actively silent.
這個計程車司機一定是頂級的。他不會主動攀談。

Crown 滴妹　 Ray 阿滴　 Joe 喬

008

 Is it just me, or is the food here just awesome? — 只有我覺得這家餐廳的食物超級好吃嗎？

 Totally. My fries are super crispy! — 我也覺得，我的薯條超級脆的！

 The steak is also perfectly grilled; it's really tender and juicy. — 牛排也煎的剛剛好，非常軟嫩又多汁。

 The service here is also top-notch. — 這裡的服務也很頂尖。

 We should come back more often. — 我們之後應該常來。

 I know right? Our food is so awesome! — 對吧對吧，我們的食物真的超讚的！

 What are you doing here, Joe? Nobody invited you. — 喬，你在這裡幹嘛？沒有人邀請你耶。

Extras

我們做過一支「吃貨必學專業美食評論」的兩分鐘英語教室，裡面教你除了 delicious 之外，五個形容食物「好吃」的方法。快掃 QR code 去看看吧！

21

餐點有問題
Excuse Me. There's a Problem

apology (n.) 抱歉

Our **apologies**. We ran out of damns to give.
很抱歉，我們真的不在乎。

notify (v.) 告知

She promised she'll **notify** me after she finished showering. It's been three months.
她上次答應我：「洗完澡再密你」，但已經過了三個月了。

make a mistake (phr.) 犯錯

I never **make** the same **mistake** twice. I make it 4-5 times just to make sure.
同樣的錯我絕對不會犯兩次。我會犯個四到五次來確認這是個錯誤。

take a bite (phr.) 嚐一口；吃

Take a bite of my burger and we're done being friends.
你敢吃我漢堡就跟你絕交。

Waiter 服務生　 Crown 滴妹　 Jane 珍

010

 Hello, Miss. How can I help you?

小姐您好，有什麼需要協助的嗎？

 Um, I think there's hair in my spaghetti...

額⋯我的義大利麵裡好像有頭髮。

 Our utmost **apologies**. Can I see where it is? We will **notify** the kitchen staff right away.

天呀，真的非常抱歉。可以讓我知道在哪嗎？我們會馬上向廚房反應。

 Also, I don't think this is what I ordered. I ordered the mushroom risotto.

不好意思，我好像也不是點這個。我點的是蘑菇燉飯。

 Let me take a look at your order for you. You're right. I **made a mistake**. The seafood paella is for table two.

我幫您確認一下。不好意思，是我搞錯了。海鮮飯是二桌的。

 By the way, I kind of **took a bite** to make sure it's not what we ordered. Hope you won't mind.

啊然後，我想確定是不是上錯所以吃了一口，希望你別介意。

 Right...

好⋯

Say It Right

「食物壞掉了」直接想到的說法可能是 The food is broken. 或是 The food is bad.。不過在英文裡面，沒有 The food is broken. 的用法，而 The food is bad. 並不是指食物壞掉了，而是指「食物很難吃」。所以當你對服務生說 The food is bad.，他可能會以為你是在批評食物難吃，而不是說食物出了問題。正確的說法是 The food has gone bad. 或者是 The food is spoilt.

23

來去速食店
At the Fast Food Restaurant

---

number (n.) 幾號餐

Crown: I'd like a **number** one, the Big Mac meal.
我要一號餐，大麥克。

Waiter: This is KFC.
這裡是肯德基。

---

double check (phr.) 再次確認

Just to **double check**, are you sure you want extra sugar in this already sugary drink?

再跟你確認一下，這飲料本身已經很甜了，你確定要點多糖？

I'm good. 沒關係。

When I say "**I'm good**", I really just mean "I don't know".

我說「沒關係」的時候，其實是在說「我不知道」。

---

counter (n.) 櫃檯

I feel most confident about my looks when I'm at the breakfast shop **counter**.

我在早餐店櫃檯時，都會對自己的美麗很有自信。

Ray 阿滴 Clerk 店員

012

 Hi, can I get a **number** seven with large fries and coke? Thanks.

嗨，我要七號餐配大薯跟可樂，謝謝。

 A Chicken McGrill meal, right?

一個板烤雞套餐對嗎？

 Wait, my bad. I wanted the Filet-o-Fish. I'll have that instead.

等下，我搞錯了。我要的是麥香魚，我要改點這個。

 Just to **double check**. A Filet-o-Fish meal with large fries and coke, right?

再跟您確認一次，您點的是麥香魚配大薯和可樂是吧？

 Yup.

對。

 Got it. Do you want some wings for $2?

好，你要加點兩塊美金的雞翅嗎？

 Nah, **I'm good.**

不用了，謝謝。

 Okay, that'll be $8. Please wait by the **counter**.

好，一共是八塊，請在櫃檯旁等候。

Say It Right

Fast food 可以指所有準備時間非常短的食物。速食餐廳之所以被稱為 fast food restaurant，除了出餐速度快、能迅速讓顧客享用到餐點之外，也是因為多數速食店使用的食材都是冷凍而且預先煮熟過的。另外，「得來速」的英文是 drive-through，仔細一唸就可以知道中文是很接近英文發音的。所以千萬不要搞錯，以為「得來速」叫做 quick-get 或是 get-quickly。

Vocabulary
主題單字

hamburger
漢堡

fries
薯條

ketchup
番茄醬

nugget
雞塊

mashed potato
馬鈴薯泥

pizza
披薩

hashbrown
薯餅

Desserts 速食店常見的甜點

pancake
鬆餅

sundae
聖代

milkshake
奶昔

Mexican Food 速食店常見的墨西哥食物

quesadilla
墨西哥餡餅

burrito
墨西哥捲餅

taco
玉米餅

tortilla
墨西哥薄餅

nacho
玉米片

07 特殊飲食需求
Special Dietary Needs

pescatarian (n.) 海鮮素主義者

I'm a **pescatarian**. Only seafood, fruits, and vegetables for me.

我吃海鮮素，只吃海鮮跟青菜水果。

pollotarian (n.) 不吃紅肉；家禽素主義者

I'm a **pollotarian**. It means I like being vegetarian, but I can't give up on my fried chicken just yet.

我不吃紅肉。意思是我喜歡當素食者，但還沒辦法不吃炸雞。

vegetarian (n.) 素食主義者

I'd be **vegetarian** if bacon grew on trees.

如果培根長在樹上的話，我就吃素。

vegan (n.) 純素食主義者

I'm so **vegan**. If I turned into a zombie, I would say 'GRAINS' instead of 'BRAINS'.

我超推純素。如果我變成殭屍，我會要稻子而不會要腦子。

Waiter 服務生 Ray 阿滴 Joe 喬

015

 Are you ready to order?

準備好要點餐了嗎？

 Yes, but I do have a small question. I know this is a steakhouse, but are there any **pescatarian** dishes on the menu?

好了，但我有個小問題。我知道這裡是牛排館，但有沒有海鮮素的餐點？

 Well, there's our special for the day. It's a seafood combo with fish fillet, pan-fried lobster, and broccoli on the side.

讓我介紹今日特餐：海鮮雙拼，有魚排和煎龍蝦，配菜是花椰菜。

 Then I'll have a special for the day, please.

太棒了，那我要一份今日特餐，謝謝。

 What about you, sir?

那這位先生呢？

 I'm sorry, but I'm a strict **vegetarian**. What would you recommend?

不好意思，我只能吃素，你會推薦什麼呢？

 You guys, this is a steakhouse.

這裡是牛排館…

Cultural Notes

在台灣的西式餐廳點餐，通常會按照菜單上的順序點餐，飲料和甜點會在最後點。但國外餐館點餐的時候，服務人員通常會先問客人：Can I start you off with anything to drink?（要先來點喝的嗎？）如果還沒有想好正餐要點什麼，可以先點飲料然後再想一下，或是直接請服務人員推薦。

29

來去星巴克
At Starbucks

caramel (n.) 焦糖

When I say that you're like **caramel**, it's used to describe how tanned you are.

當我說你像焦糖時，我是說你曬得很黑。

decaf (adj.) & (n.) 無咖啡因（的咖啡）

Decaf coffee is not real coffee. It's like wine with a 0% ABV, which is just fruity water.

無咖啡因的咖啡不是真的咖啡。就像酒精濃度為零的酒，只是有水果味的水吧。

for here (phr.) 內用

Sorry, I changed my mind. I'd like to have my meal **for here**.

不好意思，我改變主意了。我要內用。

to go (phr.) 外帶

For here or **to go**? There're no more seats available and we're fresh out of paper bags.

內用還是外帶？我們餐廳沒位子了，紙袋也剛好用完。

Ray 阿滴　　 Clerk 店員

017

 Hi, can I have an iced **caramel** macchiato, please?

你好，我要一杯冰焦糖瑪奇朵。

 Sure. What size?

沒問題，中杯大杯？

 Tall. And can you make it half sugar and **decaf**, please?

中杯的，我要半糖然後無咖啡因。

 No problem. Would you like anything else?

沒問題，還需要其他服務嗎？

 Nope, that will be all.

不用，就這樣。

 Cool, **for here** or **to go**?

好的，要內用還是外帶？

 To go, thanks.

外帶，謝謝。

Cultural Notes

星巴克常會配合季節推出特別口味，台灣的口味也常針對亞洲市場作出新嘗試，在國外也常推出一些意想不到的口味。例如在十月到一月，因應萬聖節和感恩節，會推出非常受歡迎的 Pumpkin Spice Latte（南瓜拿鐵）；冬天則是會推出有加薑餅的 Gingerbread Latte（薑餅拿鐵）。

Vocabulary
主題單字

Ordering Coffee 先點咖啡

espresso
濃縮咖啡

Americano
美式咖啡

doppio
雙倍濃縮咖啡

cold-brew
冷萃咖啡

latte
拿鐵

mocha
摩卡

frappuccino
星冰樂

Other Choices 不想喝咖啡看這裡

matcha green tea
抹茶

soybean milk
豆漿

lemonade
檸檬汁

Coffee Size 點大杯還是小杯？

8 oz/236 ml

12 oz/354 ml

16 oz/473 ml

short 小杯

tall 中杯

grande 大杯

20 oz/591 ml

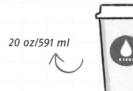

31 oz/916 ml

(only for cold drinks)

venti 特大杯

trenta 超大杯

Toppings 還可以加料

whipped cream
鮮奶油

cinnamon powder
肉桂粉

cocoa powder
可可粉

牛排幾分熟
I Want It "That" Way

ribeye (n.) 肋眼牛排

I fantasize about the perfect **ribeye** so much that I dreamt of one yesterday.
我對完美的肋眼牛排朝思暮想到我昨晚還夢到了。

tenderloin (n.) 菲力牛排

short rib (n.) 牛小排

t-bone (n.) T骨牛排

sirloin (n.) 沙朗牛排

well-done (adj.) 全熟

I said **"well-done"**, not fry it until it becomes as dry as the Sahara.
我點的是「全熟」，不是熟到像撒哈拉沙漠那樣乾掉。

rare (adj.) 一分熟

medium rare (adj.) 三分熟

medium (adj.) 五分熟

medium well (adj.) 七分熟

Crown 滴妹　　 Waiter 服務生　　 Ray 阿滴

020

 Can I get a Texan **Ribeye**, please? ┊ 請給我一份德州肋眼。

 No problem. How would you like your steak? ┊ 沒問題。請問您的牛排要幾分熟？

 Hmmm, I usually prefer **medium rare**. What would you recommend? ┊ 嗯…我通常是吃三分熟啦。你有推薦的嗎？

 Ugh, not for me, I like mine **well-done**. Thank you very much. ┊ 噢，這個我不行，我比較喜歡全熟。謝謝。

 What are you talking about? You don't even eat steak. ┊ 欸你在瞎說什麼啊？你又不能吃牛排。

 I'm just suggesting… ┊ 我只是在建議…

 Please ignore him. I'll have my ribeye medium rare. Thanks. ┊ 不要理他，我要三分熟，謝謝。

Extras

我們做過一支「牛排幾分熟」的兩分鐘英語教室，裡面有教各種形容牛排熟度的方法，快掃 QR code 去看看吧！

來去 Subway
At Subway

of the day (phr.) 本日的

Congratulations. You just won my "Least Favorite Person **of the Day**" award!

恭喜你，你獲得「本日最惹人厭」獎！

six-inch (n.) 六吋

I have such a small appetite that I can barely finish a **six-inch**.

我胃口小到連六吋潛艇堡都吃不完。

footlong (n.) 十二吋

I never get to order **footlong** because I have no friends to share it with.

我從來都不會點十二吋，因為我沒有朋友可以跟我分著吃。

sauce (n.) 醬料

Sir, if you ask for more **sauce**, I might have to charge you. You've added 5 different sauces already.

先生，你再要更多醬可能就要加錢了。你已經加了五種不同的醬料了。

Crown 滴妹　　Clerk 店員

 I'll have the Sub **of the Day**. Chicken Teriyaki.

你好，我要一個特價的照燒雞肉堡。

 Six-inch or **footlong**?

六吋還是十二吋？

 Six inch.

六吋。

 Okay, what bread would you like?

沒問題，請問你要什麼麵包？

 Parmesan Oregano, please.

巴馬乾酪，謝謝。

 Are all the veggies okay for you?

蔬菜都可以嗎？

 Yes, and I want extra jalapeños and olives.

可以，我要多一點墨西哥辣椒跟橄欖。

 And the **sauce**?

醬料呢？

 Chipotle southwest and mayo.

辣味西南醬跟美乃滋。

Cultural Notes

前陣子台灣 Subway 曾推出每日 69 元潛艇堡的優惠，而這樣的活動在國外的 Subway 則是常態，也就是「Sub of the Day」，即每日會推出優惠的口味，當天購買優惠口味十分划算。在美國，六吋的 Sub of the Day 只要三塊五美金，而十二吋則是六塊錢。比起平日絕對比較便宜。所以到國外的時候，可以看看自己喜歡的主餐口味是禮拜幾的 Sub of the Day。

Vocabulary
主題單字

Bread 先選麵包

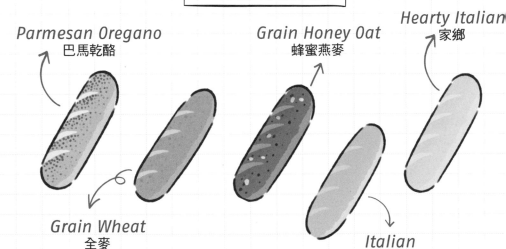

Parmesan Oregano
巴馬乾酪

Grain Honey Oat
蜂蜜燕麥

Hearty Italian
家鄉

Grain Wheat
全麥

Italian
義大利白

Flatbread
薄餅

Dressing 醬料

Chipotle Southwest
辣味西南醬

yellow mustard
黃芥末醬

mayonnaise
美乃滋醬

Vegetables 可加的蔬菜

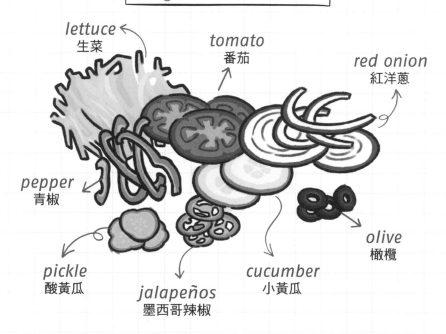

lettuce
生菜

tomato
番茄

red onion
紅洋蔥

pepper
青椒

pickle
酸黃瓜

jalapeños
墨西哥辣椒

cucumber
小黃瓜

olive
橄欖

Caesar dressing
凱薩醬

olive oil blend
橄欖油

sweet onion sauce
甜蔥醬

vinaigrette
油醋醬

11 台式早餐店怎麼點
Eating Taiwanese Breakfast

traditional (adj.) 傳統的

Judy's grandma is so **traditional** that she tried to stop her from going to school.

茱蒂的阿嬤誇張地傳統，她不讓女生接受教育。

go well with (phr.) 和…很搭

Your earrings **go well with** your overall outfit. They distract people from your face!

你的耳環跟整體服飾很搭。它讓大家不會注意到你的臉。

a variety of (phr.) 各式各樣的

We have **a variety of** goods. All of which you cannot afford.

我們有很多商品，不過你應該全部都買不起。

I'll pass. 我就算了。

Thanks for the invite, but I can't afford going sports car shopping. I think **I'll pass** this time.

謝謝你邀請我，但我實在沒錢買跑車，這次就算了吧。

Ray 阿滴  Joe 喬

025

 So, this is the **traditional** Taiwanese breakfast shop. You must try out the fried bread sticks and sesame flatbread! They **go so well with** a cup of soy milk.

這裡是傳統的台式早餐店。你一定要吃吃看燒餅跟油條！配豆漿超好吃！

 I have no idea what those things are.

我根本不知道那些是什麼東西。

 Well, breakfast in Taiwan can be very different. We have **a variety of** food you can choose from. Egg cakes are really popular...

台式早餐很不一樣，有很多種選擇。像蛋餅就滿受歡迎的…

 Egg cake? You mean like an omelet?

蛋餅？你是說蛋捲嗎？

 Not exactly, but we can always order one for you to try.

不太像，但我們可以點一份給你吃吃看。

 I'm not so sure about that. What other options are there?

我不太確定我想吃耶。還有其他選擇嗎？

 I guess the only thing left is the fried dough stick...

那就只剩油條了吧…

 Meh, I think **I'll pass**. I'll just have a burger.

嗯…還是算了吧。我吃個漢堡就好。

12 來去手搖飲料店
At the Bubble Tea Shop

bubble tea (n.) 珍珠奶茶

The chewy balls in **bubble tea** are called bobas or pearls.
珍珠奶茶裡面的珍珠英文叫做 boba 或是 pearl。

extra sugar (phr.) 多糖

Ordering **extra sugar** is a bargain. You don't get charged for the extra sweetness.
點多糖很划算。多加的那些糖都不用錢。

no ice (phr.) 去冰

I ordered **no ice** and the beverage cup came only half full.
我點了去冰，飲料來的時候只有半杯滿。

receipt (n.) 收據

Here's your **receipt** with my number written on it. Call me maybe?
這是你的收據，然後我把手機寫在上面了。打給我，好嗎？

Joe 喬   Clerk 店員 Ray 阿滴

027

 Hi, can I get a large cup of **bubble tea**, please? | 你好，我想要一杯大杯的珍珠奶茶。

 Okay, sugar and ice? | 糖和冰？

 Ray, how do people usually drink bubble milk tea? | 阿滴，大家喝珍珠奶茶通常都怎麼選？

 Well, my sister always gets **extra sugar** and **no ice.** But I wouldn't recommend that. | 額，我妹永遠都喝多糖去冰啦，但我很不建議你這樣喝。

 Okay, I think I'll have half sugar and regular ice. | 嗯，那我喝半糖正常冰好了。

 Do you need a plastic bag? It's a dollar extra. | 好，需要加一元加購塑膠袋嗎？

 No, thanks. | 不用，謝謝。

 This is your **receipt** and number. Please wait by the side. | 這裡是發票和號碼牌，旁邊稍等哦。

Cultural Notes

你知道嗎？在國外買東西領取收據的時候，會發現它很單純只是一張寫著你買了什麼的明細，並不像台灣，發票還可以拿來兌獎呦！

43

13

吃吃看！
Just Try It out!

---

night market (n.) 夜市

You can't say you've visited Taiwan if you've never been to a **night market**.

沒去過夜市，別說你來過台灣。

---

try out (phr.) 試試看

Just **try** it **out**! What's the worst thing that could happen? You'll just lose your job. That's all!

就試試看！最糟的也不過只是被炒魷魚而已啊！

---

all-time favorite (phr.) 最愛的

Fishing for compliments is my **all-time favorite** sport.

釣別人的讚美是我最愛的運動。

Now you're talking. 這樣才對嘛。

Crown: Fine. I'll clean my room up.
好啦，我會整理房間。

Ray: **Now you're talking.**
這才對嘛。

 Joe 喬　 Ray 阿滴

 Hey, Ray. Let's go to the **night market**. I heard that it's loaded with tasty Taiwanese snacks.

阿滴，我們去夜市吧！我聽說夜市有超多好吃的台灣小吃。

 Would you like to **try out** some stinky tofu first? It's known for the way it smells.

那你要先吃吃看臭豆腐嗎？它是以它的氣味出名的。

 I refuse to eat anything with the word "stinky" in it.

我拒絕吃名字裡有「臭」這個字的食物。

 It's not as bad as you think it is. Just try it out!

沒有你想得這麼糟，吃吃看嘛！

 What's that over there?

那個是什麼？

 Oyster vermicelli, one of my **all-time favorites**.

蚵仔麵線，我的最愛。

 Alright, at least that sounds like food.

好吧，至少這個聽起來像是食物。

 Now you're talking.

這才對嘛！

Say It Right

在外國影集或是電影裡有時會聽到 Now you're talking. 這句話。不知道意思的人可能會覺得，嗯？為什麼要突然說「現在你在講話」？ Now you're talking. 這句話的意思其實是「這才對嘛。」或是更詳細一點是：「天呀！你終於知道自己在講什麼了！」

Vocabulary
主題單字

fried chicken fillet
炸雞排

pearl milk tea /
bubble tea
珍珠奶茶

oyster omelet
蚵仔煎

stinky tofu
臭豆腐

braised pork rice
滷肉飯

46

steamed / fried
蒸的 / 炸的

oyster vermicelli
蚵仔麵線

Taiwanese
meatball
肉圓

braised
snacks
滷味

shaved ice
刨冰

Xiao Long Bao
小籠包

green onion
pancake
蔥油餅

暖身　十句常用購物英文

①	It's a little pricey!	這有點貴。
②	It's 10% off!	這打九折欸！
③	I'm just browsing.	我只是看看。
④	Can I try this on?	我可以試穿嗎？
⑤	Where's the fitting room?	試衣間在哪裡？
⑥	What a steal!	太划算了吧！
⑦	Do you have this in stock?	請問這有庫存嗎？
⑧	Do you take credit cards?	可以刷卡嗎？
⑨	Can I have a refund?	可以退費嗎？
⑩	I would like to speak to the manager.	叫經理出來。

取自 YouTube
購物衣服篇

031

今天該穿什麼
Outfit of the Day

try on (phr.) 試穿

Whenever I **try on** the clothes I bought online, I curse the models that fooled me into buying them.

每次試穿網購的衣服，就會詛咒那些騙我下單的模特兒們。

blouse (n.) 女用襯衫

I'm going to my ex's party wearing a low-cut **blouse**, just to remind him that he's missing out.

我要穿低胸襯衫參加前男友的派對，讓他知道他錯過了什麼。

throw on (phr.) 隨意穿上

I'll just **throw on** my red underwear for the cosplay party tonight. Superman for the win!

今晚的變裝派對我就穿個紅內褲去好了。超人最棒了！

pajamas (n.) 睡衣

I secretly keep my boyfriend's **pajamas** in zip-lock bags so that I can take them out for occasional whiffs.

我會偷偷把男友睡衣放在夾鏈袋裡，不時打開來聞一下。

Crown 滴妹

Ray 阿滴

032

 Hmm…What should I wear to the YouTuber convention today?

嗯…要穿什麼去 YouTuber 大會呢？

 Crown, we're leaving in 30 minutes.

滴妹，我們三十分鐘後 出發哦！

 I should **try on** that dress I bought. Oh wait, was it a **blouse** instead?

噢！穿我上次買的洋裝 好了。噢等等，還是我 買的是襯衫？

 Crown, ten minutes! Hurry up!

滴妹，還有十分鐘！快 一點！

 Almost ready! Okay, time's up. I'll just **throw on** a t-shirt and my jeans. Easy.

快好了！好，我穿 T 恤 跟牛仔褲好了。輕鬆簡 單。

 Crown! What's taking so long? What are you wearing?

滴妹！你到底在幹嘛？ 你穿的是什麼？

 My **pajamas**. Everything else is in the laundry, so I had no choice.

我的睡衣啊，其他衣服 都在洗，所以沒什麼可 以穿了…

 …

…

Extras

我們有做過一支「衣服」的日常單字影片，裡面教你各種 不同衣服的說法，快掃 QR code 去看看吧！

刷卡還是付現
Cash or Credit?

check out (phr.) 結帳

Whenever I buy video games, I ask my friend to **check them out** so that I don't look like a nerd.

我買遊戲的時候都會叫我朋友結帳，這樣我才不會看起來很宅。

buy one get one free (phr.) 買一送一

You can't just say no to **buy one get one free.** You buy one and you get another one for free!

你不能不要買一送一！因為你買一個就會多送一個啊！

credit (card) (n.) 信用卡

Credit cards are like magic; only that they come back to haunt you a month later.

信用卡就像是魔術一樣。只不過是一個月之後會回來找你算帳。

cash (n.) 現金

Don't talk to me about your company vision. Just show me the **cash.**

不要跟我說公司的遠景，讓我賺錢就好。

Crown 滴妹 Clerk 店員
034

 Hi, I'd like to **check** these **out**, please. | 你好，我要結帳。

 No problem. Did you find everything you needed? | 沒問題，有找到你需要的東西嗎？

 I sure did! | 有哦有哦！

 This is a **buy one get one free** item. Can you pick out another one over there? | 這個買一送一，你能從那邊再選一件嗎？

 Oh, okay. I'll take the pink one, please. | 好啊，我要粉紅色的。

 Would you like a bag for all your clothes? | 需要袋子裝嗎？

 Yes, please. | 好啊。

 That's $60.49 altogether. **Cash** or **credit**? | 這樣是 60.49 元，請問刷卡還是付現？

 Credit. Thanks. | 刷卡，謝謝。

 Here's your receipt. Have a nice day! | 這邊是明細，謝謝光臨！

035

衣服太多
Throw out Your Clothes!

clear out (phr.) 清理

I really need to **clear out** my desk. I can't even see its surface.

我真的需要清理一下桌子，我連桌面都看不見了。

delivery (n.) 運送

The **delivery** has such bad timing. It's like they know exactly when I'm not home and choose to visit during that time.

快遞來的時間都很怪，好像他們能精準知道我哪時候不在家，然後故意在那個時段送來。

throw (v.) 丟

Is it rude to **throw** a breath mint in someone's mouth while they are talking?

如果一個人講話到一半我把薄荷糖丟到他嘴巴裡面，會很失禮嗎？

recycle (v.) 回收

I bet you're really good at **recycling** because you're pure garbage.

你回收一定做得很好，因為你本人就是個垃圾。

Ray 阿滴　 Crown 滴妹

 Crown, stop shopping online! I already **cleared out** half of my closet for your clothes.

滴妹，不要再網購了！我都已經讓出一半的衣櫃給你放了！

 I ordered these three months ago! It's not my fault they have slow **delivery**!

這些是我三個月前買的，貨比較慢到又不是我的錯！

 That's it. You're cleaning your room today.

我受夠了，你今天要整理房間。

 What? No!

什麼？我不要！

 I'm going to watch you **throw** out all the clothes you don't wear. Like this one.

我要看著你把沒在穿的衣服丟掉，像這件。

 That's my favorite sweater!

這是我最喜歡的毛衣欸！

 It's summer! Plus, when was the last time you wore it?

都夏天了！而且你上次穿是什麼時候？

 Um…Half a year ago?

呃…半年前？

 It's going in the **recycling**. Start cleaning, otherwise I'll do it for you.

回收！開始整理，不然我就幫妳全丟了。

Say It Right

clean 跟 clear 這兩個字雖然長得很類似，但意思有些不同。clean 是指「打掃、弄乾淨」，雖然 clear 也有清理的意思，但它另一個解釋是「清空」。所以如果你是要把東西清空，用 clear something out 表達，會比 clean 還來得精準。

55

Summer Clothing 夏天衣物

blouse
女用短袖上衣

crop top
短版背心

tank top
背心

bra
胸罩

T-shirt
T 恤

shirt
襯衫

underwear
內褲

jeans
牛仔褲

037

Winter Clothing 冬天衣物

jumper
針織套衫

sweater
毛衣

vest
背心

jacket
夾克

cardigan
開襟羊毛衫

hoodie
帽T

stockings
長襪

leggings
內搭褲

socks
短襪

網購衣服
Online Shopping

---

free shipping (n.) 免運

Why yes, I would spend $300 more to get **free shipping** to avoid paying $30 for shipping.

真棒，我可以多花三百元湊到免運，這樣就不用花三十元運費了。

---

clearance (n.) 清倉

It's **clearance** season. I'm prepared to starve for the rest of the month.

現在是清倉季，我準備好這個月吃土了。

---

come in one's size (phr.) 是某人的尺寸

Just because it **comes in your size** doesn't mean you should wear it. You look ridiculous in that skirt.

有你的尺寸不等於適合你，你穿這件裙子看起來很荒謬。

---

impulse (n.) 衝動

Every **impulse** to quit your job can be soothed, once you take a look at your credit card bills.

只要看看信用卡帳單，想離職的衝動就可以平息下來。

 Oh my gosh! **Free shipping** worldwide? Christmas is early this year! | 我的天啊！全球免運費！聖誕節提早來了嗎？

 What are you doing? | 你在幹嘛？

 UNIQLO is holding an online **clearance** and on top of that, free shipping worldwide! | UNIQLO 線上大出清！重點是，全球免運！

 Oh, no. I have a bad feeling about this. | 我有不祥的預感…

 Do you think this cashmere sweater would look good on me? What about this cute pair of shorts? | 你覺得我穿這件喀什米爾毛衣好看嗎？這條可愛的短褲呢？

 Crown… | 滴妹…

 This is the dress I wanted to buy last winter! And it still **comes in my size**! | 這件裙子是我去年冬天想買的！而且還有我的尺寸！

 Crown! The sale doesn't start until next month! Open up your eyes before shopping on **impulse**! | 滴妹！特賣下個月才開始！衝動購物前先看清楚好嗎？

選購飾品
Shopping for Accessories

occasion (n.) 特殊場合或日子

What's the **occasion**? You're not a total prick today.

今天是什麼日子啊？你怎麼忽然人這麼好？

anniversary (n.) 紀念日

I didn't forget our **anniversary.** I just forgot that it's today.

我沒有忘記我們的紀念日啊，我只是忘記是今天。

pick out (phr.) 挑選

I would love to help you **pick out** which summer clothes you're not allowed to wear anymore.

我很樂意幫你挑選出來你以後都不能再穿的夏天衣服。

gift-wrapped (adj.) 以禮盒包裝的

The thing I love most about your gift is that it's **gift-wrapped.**

我最喜歡你禮物的部分是包裝。

Clerk 店員 **Ray** 阿滴

 How may I help you today?　　　　需要什麼幫忙嗎？

 I'm looking for a simple necklace, meant for someone else.

我想要找一個簡單的項鍊，要送人的。

 Is it for a special **occasion**? An **anniversary** perhaps?

是為了什麼特殊場合嗎？紀念日？

 Oh, no. It's not for anything special.

喔沒有，沒什麼特別的需求。

 Do you need some recommendations? Or do you want to **pick** it **out** yourself?

你需要我推薦嗎？還是想要自己選？

 I'm just browsing.

我只是看看。

 No problem. I'm here if you need me.

沒問題，需要都可以找我。

 Can I take a look at that silver one over there?

我可以看一下那邊那個銀色的嗎？

 Sure! Do you need it **gift-wrapped**? It's free of charge.

沒問題！你需要禮盒包裝嗎？免費的喔。

 Dude, hold on. I haven't decided yet.

欸等等啊，我還沒決定好啊。

Please buy it. My bonus depends on it.

拜託你買，我的獎金就靠這個了。

61

Accessories 配件

suspenders
吊帶

handkerchief
手帕

belt
皮帶

earmuffs
耳罩

scarf
圍巾

mittens
連指手套

gloves
手套

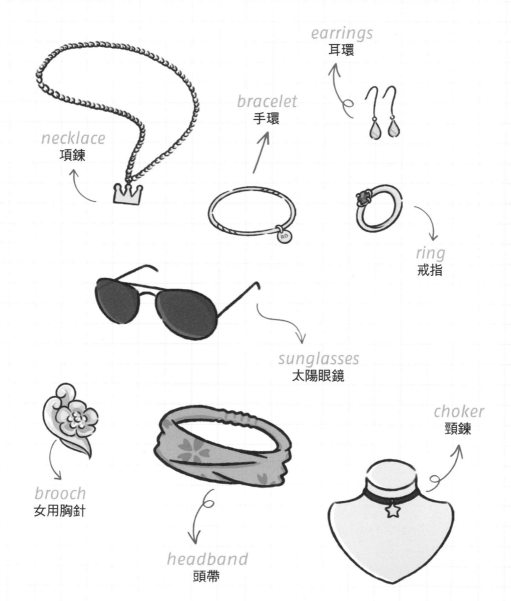

earrings
耳環

bracelet
手環

necklace
項鍊

ring
戒指

sunglasses
太陽眼鏡

choker
頸鍊

brooch
女用胸針

headband
頭帶

稱讚 / 批評穿搭
You Look Nice

look good on (phr.) 適合、耐看

Everything **looks good on** internet celebrities, but when I put on the same piece, I immediately regret my purchase.

在網美身上什麼衣服都很適合，但當我穿上一樣的衣服時，我馬上後悔自己腦波弱。

match (v.) 搭

You should find a pretty face to **match** yours. For example, mine.

你要找個顏值高的才配得上你，比如說我。

plaid (n.) 格紋

I told you not to wear your orange **plaid** shirt to the job interview…

我就跟你說了，工作面試不要穿那件橘色的格子襯衫…

baggy (adj.) 鬆垮的

Your **baggy** hoodie really compliments your chubby face.

你鬆垮的帽 T 真的跟你圓圓的臉很搭。

Crown 滴妹 Ray 阿滴

 Does this **look good on** me? | 這件適合我嗎？

 The colors don't **match**. | 顏色不搭。

 What do you think of this **plaid** shirt? | 你覺得這個格子襯衫怎麼樣？

 You look like a zebra. | 你看起來像斑馬。

 Do you think I should wear a jacket? | 你覺得我要不要穿件外套？

 It's too **baggy**. You look miserable. | 太垮，你看起來很糟。

 Do I look fat in this? | 我這樣看起來很胖嗎？

 That's the most difficult question to answer in the entire universe. | 這問題宇宙難回答。

Say It Right

常見的衣服花紋有這幾種：stripe（直條）、checked（棋盤格紋）、floral（花）、leopard（豹紋）、polka dot（點點）、zebra（斑馬紋）。

 選購化妝品
Shopping for Beauty Products

foundation (n.) 粉底；基礎

My cosmetic bag has a better **foundation** than our relationship.

我化妝包裡的粉底（基礎）比我們之間的關係還要好。

range (n.) 範圍

Facebook is testing the emotional **range** of page owners worldwide by reducing organic reach to oblivion.

臉書透過腰斬自然觸及，測試全球粉絲專頁小編的心臟強度。

moisturize (v.) 濕潤

Drinking 10 bottles of water a day will not help **moisturize** your skin. You'll just pee a lot.

一天喝 10 瓶水不會幫你肌膚補水，只會讓你一直跑廁所。

skin tone (n.) 膚色

By improving my **skin tone,** I mean that I want to stay at home all day, every day.

我說想要改善我的膚色意思是，我要天天宅在家裡不出門。

Clerk 店員  Crown 滴妹

046

 Hello, welcome to Sephora. Are you looking for anything in particular?

你好，歡迎光臨 Sephora，有特別要找什麼嗎？

 I'm actually looking for **foundation**. Any recommendations?

我在找粉底，有推薦的嗎？

 A lot of brands offer wide foundation **ranges**. Would you like to try them out?

很多品牌都有滿多色號選擇的，要試試嗎？

 I'm just looking for something that's more **moisturizing**.

好啊，我想找比較保濕一點的。

 Alright. So if you'll just try this one out for me.

好，那你幫我試試看這一款。

 Hmm, I think this is a bit too pale for my **skin tone**.

嗯…我覺得這個對我的膚色來說太白了。

 How about this one?

那這個呢？

 Perfect! I'll take it, thanks!

很好！我就買這個了，謝謝！

 No problem at all. I hope you find everything okay at Sephora!

沒問題，祝你在 Sephora 消費愉快！

Vocabulary
主題單字

Foundation 底妝

primer
妝前乳

foundation
粉底

concealer
遮瑕膏

Contour 修容

highlight
打亮

blush
腮紅

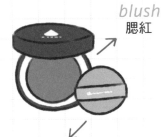

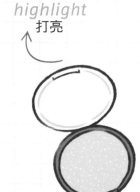

bronzer
古銅餅

powder puff
粉撲

contour
修容餅

Eye Makeup 眼部彩妝

eyeliner
眼線筆

mascara
睫毛膏

eye shadow
眼影

Lip Makeup 唇部彩妝

Others 其他

lipstick
唇膏

perfume
香水

nail polish
指甲油

lip balm
護唇膏

deodorant
止汗劑

lotion
乳液

回家洗衣服 / 燙衣服

Laundry Day

hang out (phr.) 約一下、出來聚聚

Let's **hang out** tonight, and by hang out I mean get drunk.
我們今晚來約約吧，然後我說約的意思是一起喝醉。

laundry (n.) 要洗的衣服

I finished your **laundry**. The ashes are in the fireplace.
我把你的髒衣服搞定了，灰燼都在壁爐裡。

iron (v.) 燙衣服

The only time I **iron** my own clothes was never.
我唯一一次自己燙過衣服是其實一次都沒有。

plenty (adj.) 很多的

You've got **plenty** of time to figure out what you want to have for lunch. I'll just leave you to it.
你有很多時間可以想午餐到底要吃什麼。先走囉，你慢慢想。

Jane 珍　 Crown 滴妹

 Hey, Crown. Wanna **hang out** tonight?

嘿，滴妹，晚上要不要出去玩？

 Um, I can't. I have to go home and do **laundry**. So I'll be hanging out laundry.

不行欸…我要回家洗衣服。我跟衣服有約。

 Okay, what about this weekend? We can go for a picnic.

那這週末呢？我們可以去野餐。

 On weekends, I have to **iron** my shirts for work.

我週末還得燙工作要穿的襯衫。

 Fine. Maybe next week?

好吧，那下禮拜呢？

 Um…

嗯…

 Come on! How many clothes do you have that need washing?

拜託！你是有多少衣服要洗？

 Haven't you seen that video of my room? Let's just say, I've got **plenty**.

你沒看過我房間的影片嗎？我只能說，超多。

Cultural Notes

把衣服晾在戶外感覺是在普通也不過的事情，但在美國某些州，如果把衣服晾在外面，可是會犯法的喔！據說當地有些人認為，把衣服曬在戶外會影響社區整體美觀，而使得房價下跌，所以設立相關法令，禁止把衣服晾在戶外。

71

09 辦理退貨 / 退款
Asking for Return or Refund

return (v.) & (n.) 退貨

Can I **return** this underwear? It's a bit small. I have never worn it. I swear.

我可以退這條內褲嗎？有點小，但我還沒有穿過，我保證。

fit (v.) 合身

I ate so much tonight that my jeans don't **fit** anymore.

我今晚吃超多，牛仔褲變超緊。

exchange (v.) 換貨

Don't go back to the store to **exchange** your present. You won't believe how little I spent on it.

不要把我送你的禮物拿回去店裡換，你會無法相信我有多小氣。

tag (n.) 標籤

That dude forgot to lose the **tag** and now we know that he's wearing a $200 T-shirt.

那位老兄忘記把標籤剪掉，現在我們都知道他的 T 恤兩百塊。

Ray 阿滴   Clerk 店員

051

 I bought these sweatpants here last week. I'd like to **return** them, please?

我上禮拜在這裡買了這件棉褲，可以退貨嗎？

 OK, let's see what I can do. Do you have your receipt?

好，我來看一下。你有帶收據嗎？

 Sure, here you go.

有喔，在這裡。

 May I ask why you want to return them?

可以問你為什麼想退貨嗎？

 They don't **fit** me really well. They're a bit too baggy.

這個尺寸不太對，有點太垮了。

 OK. Did you just want to **exchange** them for a different size?

好，還是說你想要換一件不同尺寸的？

 But come to think of it, I already own 10 sweatpants. I don't think I need another one.

但其實，我家裡已經有 10 件棉褲了，我應該不用再多一件了。

 OK... so you'd like a refund?

好…所以你想退費嗎？

 Yeah, if that's OK. All the **tags** are still on the sweatpants. I didn't wear them at all.

對，如果可以的話。所有的標籤都沒有剪，我也沒穿過喔。

Say It Right

英文字裡常見的字首之一就是「re-」，這個字首帶有兩種不同的含義。第一種含義是「再一次」或是「一而再再而三」，例如 review（複習）和 repeat（重複）。第二種含義則是「返回」或是「倒退」，例如對話中的 return（退回）以及 refund（退款）。

選購鞋子
Shopping for Shoes

---

shopping spree (n.) 瘋狂購物

My rich friend buys houses on his **shopping spree**.
I buy trousers.

我的富二代朋友在瘋狂購物時是買房子。我的話是買褲子。

---

casual (adj.) 休閒的

Your Batman costume does not qualify as business **casual**.
Not by a long shot.

你的蝙蝠俠套裝不算是休閒上班服裝。完全不算。

---

shoe size (n.) 鞋子尺寸

In astrological fortune telling, your **shoe size** has a certain
correlation to your longevity, not.

在星座運勢裡，你的鞋子大小跟壽命會有關聯，才怪。

---

in a ... (size) (phr.) 某某大小的

When I shop for shoes, my favorite colors always come **in
a size** that's a bit smaller or larger than what I needed.

我每次買鞋子的時候，最喜歡的顏色總是太大或太小。

Crown 滴妹 Ray 阿滴

053

 Ray, your birthday's coming up. I want to get you something.

哥,你生日要到了,我想買禮物給你。

 You don't have to. But just so you know, I happen to need a new pair of shoes…

不用啦,不過,我最近剛好需要一雙新鞋…

 A new pair of shoes it is. Let's go to the mall.

那就買一雙新鞋啊!我們去逛百貨公司吧!

 I hope this is not one of your **shopping sprees**…

希望你不要又密謀要瘋狂採購…

 What are you talking about? We're here shopping for you! So what's it gonna be?

你在講什麼?我們是來幫你買東西的!所以你要買什麼?

 Hmm, I'm looking for something comfortable and **casual**.

嗯嗯,我想買穿起來舒服然後休閒的。

 Maybe a pair of loafers? What's your **shoe size**?

懶人鞋如何?你鞋子穿幾號?

 I think I need them **in a 10**. But I'll try them on to make sure.

我應該是美碼 10 號。但是我要試穿才能確定。

 Got it. Let's just go to the cosmetics counter just to give you some other options.

了解,那我們去美妝區吧,讓你知道你還可以買什麼。

Cultural Notes

每個國家都有自己測量鞋子大小的單位及方法,台灣習慣使用公分 (cm),但歐美品牌卻又有分 US 或 UK 等等。雖然有些 outlet 會在牆上掛各個尺碼的換算,但最好的辦法還是知道自己穿什麼尺寸,不然真的只能一雙一雙試穿啦!

Vocabulary
主題單字

Shoes 鞋子種類

flats
平底鞋

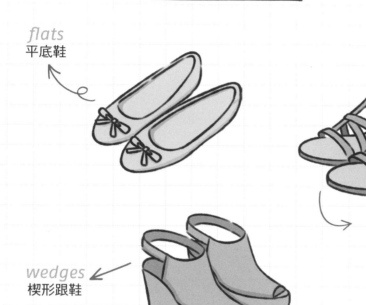

sandals
涼鞋

wedges
楔形跟鞋

heels
高跟鞋

stilettos
細跟高跟鞋

shoelace
鞋帶

loafers
樂福鞋（平底船鞋）

boots
靴子

sneakers
運動鞋

cleats
釘鞋

slippers
拖鞋

flip-flops
夾腳拖

clogs
木屐

暖身　十句常用飯店英文

①	How can I help you?	我可以怎麼協助你？
②	Do you have a reservation?	你有訂房嗎？
③	Do you want a single or a double room?	你需要單人還是雙人房？
④	Could I see some ID, please?	可以給我看證件嗎？
⑤	Your room is 9487.	你的房間是 9487。
⑥	Could you fill out this form?	可以幫我填這個表格嗎？
⑦	Your room includes breakfast.	你的訂房附有早餐。
⑧	Check out is before 12 p.m.	中午 12 點前要退房。
⑨	Is there anything else I can do for you?	還有什麼需要協助的嗎？
⑩	We look forward to seeing you again.	期待您再次光臨。

取自 YouTube
飯店入住篇

01 尋找適合的訂房
Finding a Place to Stay

book (v.) 預訂

My first day back at work has inspired me to **book** my next vacation.

受到開工的啟發，我就排了下一次休假。

downtown (n.) 市中心

Our apartment is just a few blocks away from **downtown**! And by a few blocks I mean a 50-minute drive.

我們的公寓離市中心只有幾條街喔！然後我的幾條街意思是要開車五十分鐘。

on a budget (phr.) 預算有限

Our company is running **on a** tight **budget**. We secretly use our neighbor's Wi-Fi signal.

我們公司的預算很緊。連 Wi-Fi 都是偷用鄰居的。

high rating (n.) 評價很高

This app has **high ratings** if you ignore the fact that most comments are left by spam bots.

這個 APP 的評價很高，如果你忽略評分的留言感覺都是機器人這件事。

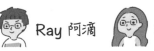

 We have a trip coming up. Did you **book** our rooms yet?

我們就要出國了，你房間訂了嗎？

 We can get it done right now. What's the duration of our stay?

我們可以現在搞定。我們是哪幾天去？

 May 6th to 13th. So we'll need a place to stay for a whole week.

5/6 到 5/13，所以我們需要找一個禮拜的住宿。

 And we'll be 2 adults in 1 room…are we looking for hotels or bnbs?

兩個大人，一個房間…我們要找飯店還是民宿？

 I think we can do bed and breakfast, preferably in the **downtown** area.

我覺得可以找民宿，最好是在市區。

 Here's a couple that looks promising. The average price is around $6000 per night.

這裡有幾個看起來很不錯。平均價錢落在六千元一晚。

 We're **on a budget**. Can you filter to the ones around $3000?

那有點超出預算。你可以設定價錢在三千元左右的嗎？

 Sure, but most are in the suburbs. Is that okay?

可以啊，但是幾乎都在市區外圍，可以嗎？

 Yeah, I'm sure public transportation works pretty well there. We should be okay.

嗯，那裡的交通蠻方便的。應該沒問題。

 How about this one? It's got **high ratings** overall and well within our budget.

那這個呢？它的整體評價蠻高的，也完全在預算內。

 Sure, let's book it and contact the host for further information.

好啊，我們先訂下來，然後再跟房東聯繫吧。

Vocabulary
主題單字

Places to Stay 住宿類型

**RV
(recreational vehicle)**
旅遊車

tent
帳篷

hostel
旅舍

resort
度假村

inn
客棧

motel
汽車旅館

bnb
（*bed and breakfast*）
民宿

hotel
飯店

Different Housing 住房類型

townhouse
連排房屋

apartment
公寓

penthouse
頂層豪華公寓

suite
套房

cottage
農舍小屋

igloo
冰屋

villa
別墅

mansion
豪宅

83

跟房東租房
Renting a House

---

furnished (adj.) 配備傢俱的

Oh, you are planning to keep a cat in your fully-**furnished** new house? Good luck.

喔，你想要在你剛裝潢好的新房養貓嗎？祝好運。

---

rent (n.) 房租

Can I pay my **rent** in the form of autographs? They are worth a lot of money (not).

我可以用簽名照付房租嗎？它們很值錢的（才怪）。

---

up front (phr.) 提前付款

I'm not paying $1000 **up front** for a book club I won't attend.

我才不要預付一千元參加一個我根本不會去的讀書會。

---

utilities (n.) 公共設施（水電等）

I forgot to pay the bills for **utilities** and now I'm stuck in the dark with no water to shower.

忘記繳水電費了，害我現在摸黑又沒水可以洗澡。

Landlord 房東　 Ray 阿滴

 As you can see, the apartment is fully **furnished**. I just got it renovated three years ago, so everything is relatively new.

如你所見，這個公寓是有完整傢俱設備的。我三年前才剛整修過，所以一切都蠻新的。

 The place looks great! It's really spacious, too. How much is the **rent**?

這裡看起來很棒！也很寬敞。租金是多少？

 I'll let you have it for $40000 a month.

我算你一個月四萬。

 Oh, I don't think I can afford that on my own. Is it okay if I find a roommate?

我一個人可能無法負擔得起，可以找室友嗎？

 That's fine. No pets though.

可以有室友，但不能養寵物。

 Got it. If you don't mind me asking, what do I need to prepare so that I can move in?

沒問題。如果你不介意的話，我想問，如果要搬進來需要先準備什麼東西？

 To move in, you need to pay two month's rent in advance plus a safety deposit.

搬進來前你需要先支付兩個月的租金加上一些押金。

 Okay, so that's about $100000 **up front**. What about water and electricity?

OK，所以差不多是要先預付十萬元。那水費跟電費呢？

On average, the **utilities** would cost you around $3000 a month.

水電費每個月平均會是三千元。

 Alright, thanks for the info! I'll sleep on it and get back to you!

好的。謝謝您的導覽！我想一想再跟您聯繫。

辦理入住
Checking in at the Hotel

check in (phr.) 辦理住宿手續

Our flight delayed and we had to **check in** at the hotel last minute.

我們的飛機誤點，導致我們趕在最後一刻才到飯店辦入住。

include (v.) 包含

Perks of working at Ray Du English Studio **include** seeing Ray every day and seeing Ray every day.

在阿滴英文工作室工作的好處包含每天看到阿滴和每天看到阿滴。

stay (n.) & (v.) 停留、逗留

I was so homesick that I drank bubble tea every day during my **stay** in the UK.

我想家想到在英國的每一天都要來杯珍珠奶茶。

sleep in (phr.) 睡到很晚起床

Ray gets up early every day, whereas I **sleep in** until noon.

阿滴每天都很早起，然而我每天都睡到中午。

Crown 滴妹   Front Desk 櫃檯

061

 Hello, I have a room reserved. I'd like to **check in**, please.

你好，我有預定一間房間，我想要辦入住。

 May I have your passport and credit card, please?

麻煩請出示護照及信用卡。

 Here you go.

這邊。

 Welcome to Continental Hotel, Ms. Du. You have a room reserved. Two single beds for three nights, is that correct?

都小姐，歡迎來到洲際飯店，您預定了一間房間，兩張單人床，三個晚上。請問正確嗎？

 Yes, and I'm wondering if breakfast is **included**.

對，然後我想知道有沒有包含早餐？

 Breakfast is included during your **stay** here and is served between 7 a.m. to 11 a.m.

您入住的期間有包含早餐，用餐時間早上七點到十一點。

 Awesome! I'll be able to **sleep in** and not worry about not having the most important meal of the day.

太棒了，我睡晚一點也不用擔心沒吃到一天中最重要的一餐。

 Right…Your room number is 1027 and here's your room card. Enjoy your stay at Continental!

好哦…您的房間號碼是1027，這邊是您的房卡。祝您住宿愉快！

Cultural Notes

在國外，除了吃飯要給小費（tip），住飯店也要給小費！以美金來說，通常一個晚上是給一塊錢。而且切記，不管到哪裡，小費都不要給硬幣！小費放置的位子以明顯為主，例如枕頭上、床頭櫃，或是小茶几。

詢問飯店設施
Hotel Facilities

facility (n.) 設施

I don't need a room with kitchen **facility**. I can't cook.

我不需要有廚房設備的房間，我不會煮飯。

complimentary (adj.) 贈送的

The airline offered a **complimentary** upgrade for accidentally cancelling my ticket. They gave me an extra blanket.

航空公司因為不小心取消了我的機票而免費幫我升級，他們多給了我一條毯子。

toiletries (n.) 盥洗用品

Why do you need extra **toiletries**? You don't even shower.

你為啥需要額外的盥洗用品？你又沒在洗澡。

charge (v.) 向…收費

I can't believe that shop **charged** me $50 for a bottle of water. Robbery!

我不敢相信那家店竟然賣我一罐五十元的礦泉水。搶劫啊！

Ray 阿滴　 Front Desk 櫃檯

063

 Hi, I just checked into my room and I have some questions about the **facilities**.

你好，我剛辦了入住，但我想問一些跟設施有關的問題。

 How can I help you, sir?

我能怎麼協助您？

 Um, is the bottled water in the room **complimentary**?

房間裡的水是送的嗎？

 Yes, it is. And if you need more, you can always call room service.

是的。如果您還有需要的話，可以打客房服務。

 Nice! How about the **toiletries**, will you **charge** me if I ask for more?

讚哦！那盥洗用品的話，如果我要更多的話需要收費嗎？

 Due to environmental causes, we do not offer extra toiletries for free.

為了響應環保，我們不會額外提供免費的盥洗用品。

 Understood. I read somewhere that you have a gym available for guests? Which floor is it on?

了解，我有看到介紹說這裡有運動中心？是在幾樓？

 My apologies. The gym is under renovation right now, so it's not accessible.

不好意思，運動中心現在正在施工中，目前無法使用。

Cultural Notes

並不是所有國外飯店都會每天幫你整理房間。尤其現在環保意識抬頭，許多飯店也不會天天為房客更換毛巾以及棉被。若有需要，可以向服務台詢問。

Vocabulary
主題單字

Hotel Facilities 飯店設施

swimming pool
游泳池

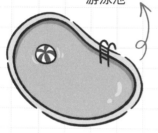

fitness center
健身中心

dumbbell
啞鈴

bartender
調酒師

bar
酒吧

laundry
洗衣房

vending machine
販賣機

conference room
會議室

Hotel Services 飯店服務

airport shuttle
機場接送

Wi-Fi
無線網路

dry-cleaning
乾洗

wake-up call
電話叫醒服務

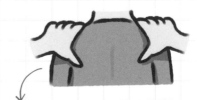

massage
按摩

客房服務
Room Service

run out of (phr.) 用完、耗盡

Will you please hurry up? We're **running out of** time!
你動作可以快一點嗎？我們快沒時間了

suggest (v.) 建議

I **suggest** we drink before going to the bar!
我提議去酒吧之前就先喝一杯吧！

staff (n.) 職員

The **staff** meeting scheduled at 9: 00 will begin promptly at 9: 45.
表定九點的員工會議會在九點四十五分準時開始。

in a moment (phr.) 馬上、立刻

I'll be with you **in a moment**, but if it's past 6, there's no way I'll work overtime for you.
我等等就去找你。但如果超過六點，我絕對不會加班。

Crown 滴妹 Operator 總機

 Hi, can I order something from the kitchen?

嗨，我可以從廚房點一些東西上來吃嗎？

 Of course, what can I get you?

沒問題，您想吃什麼？

 Can I have the crab sandwich, the filet mignon, and some fries?

我想要螃蟹三明治、菲力牛排，跟一些薯條。

 Sorry, but we **ran out of** the filet. May I **suggest** the porterhouse?

不好意思，菲力沒有了。您可以考慮紅屋牛排。

 I can't seem to find it on the menu…

我在菜單上找不太到…

 It should be on the next page.

應該是在下一頁。

 Okay, I see it. Sure, I'll have the porterhouse instead.

OK，我看到了。好，那我就換一份紅屋牛排。

 Will that be all?

這樣就好了嗎？

 Yes, thank you.

是的，謝謝。

 Okay, our **staff** will bring you your food **in a moment**. Bye.

我們的同仁會盡快為您送上餐點。再見。

067

更換房間
Changing Rooms

spare (adj.) 多餘的

Are there any **spare** batteries? I really need to get back to *The Legend of Zelda*.

有多的電池嗎？我得趕快繼續打《薩爾達傳說》。

available (adj.) 可用的

The ball pit is not **available** right now because some kid left his diaper inside and we're looking for it.

球池現在不開放，裡面有個小孩的尿布，我們現在在找。

flooding (adj.) 淹水的；充滿的

YouTube is **flooding** with clickbait videos. I'm so sick of it! I should start doing it, too.

YouTube 一堆騙點擊的影片，好煩！我應該也要這樣做。

haunted (adj.) 鬧鬼的

I think Crown's room is **haunted**. Every time I clean it, it just gets messy by itself the next day.

我覺得滴妹的房間鬧鬼。每次我整理乾淨之後它都會自動變亂。

Ray 阿滴　 Front Desk 櫃檯

068

 Excuse me. Are there any **spare** rooms **available** tonight?

不好意思，請問今天晚上還有其他空房嗎？

 Is there something wrong with your room? I'm afraid there are no other vacant rooms for the night.

您的房間有什麼問題嗎？今晚恐怕已經沒有別的空房了。

 Well, I think someone's smoking in the room down the hall.

是嗎？我覺得有人在走廊盡頭的房間抽菸。

 Our hotel is strictly smoke-free. We will have someone notify them right away.

我們飯店是嚴禁吸菸的，我們會馬上請人通知他們。

 The sink is also broken, and the entire bathroom is **flooding**.

還有我的水槽好像壞了，整個廁所都在淹水。

 Really? In that case, we'll have our staff look into that immediately.

真的嗎？那我馬上派人去看看。

 The remote control for the air-con is also broken. It doesn't work.

然後冷氣遙控器也壞了。沒反應。

 Anything else?

還有嗎？

 And finally, I think the room is **haunted**. The light keeps flickering and I hear weird voices coming out of the speakers.

我其實覺得房間不乾淨。電燈一直閃，然後喇叭會傳出奇怪的聲音。

 I'll get you a new room.

我幫你換房間。

07 辦理退房
Checking out at the Hotel

check out (phr.) 辦理退房手續

When they say we have to **check out** before 11, I thought they meant 11 p.m.

他們說十一點前要退房，我以為他們指的是晚上十一點。

additional (adj.) 額外的

I can't believe they charged me an **additional** $50 for "accidentally" drinking another bottle of water.

我不敢相信他們因為我「不小心」喝了另外一罐水而跟我多收五十塊。

form (n.) 表格

After filling out this **form** and paying the outrageous application fee, I'll be able to tell you how you will succeed in life.

填完這個表格然後付完超高的申請費後，我就可以告訴你未來會怎麼成功喔！

claim (v.) 認領、索取

I'm here to **claim** my brother. You just called and said he got lost in the women's clothing section.

我來領我哥的，你們剛打來說他在女裝區迷路了。

Crown 滴妹　 Front Desk 櫃檯

 I'd like to **check out**, please.

我想要退房,謝謝。

 Okay, can I have your room key, please? Did you have a pleasant time at Continental?

好的,請將房卡交回。在洲際酒店住宿期間都還滿意嗎?

 Yeah, the room was really nice and the bed was comfortable.

很好,房間很棒而且床也很舒服。

 I just doubled checked and you have no **additional** charges for your stay. We look forward to seeing you at Continental again.

剛剛確認過您住宿期間沒有任何額外的消費,我們期待您能再次蒞臨洲際酒店。

 Is it possible to leave our luggage here before we head to the airport? We still have a few places we want to visit.

請問我們去機場之前能先把行李寄放在這嗎?我們還有些想去的景點。

 No problem. Just fill out this **form** and the name tag. We will put them in our baggage storage.

沒問題,請幫我填寫這份表格和名牌。我們會將您的行李放在行李房。

 And we can **claim** our luggage based on the tags?

然後我們用名牌領回,是嗎?

 That is correct.

沒錯。

① I'm going to New York. 　　我要去紐約。

② Here you go. 　　給你。

③ Window seat, please. 　　請給我靠窗的位子。

④ Just this one. 　　就這個而已。

⑤ Is my baggage overweight? 　　我的行李超重了嗎？

⑥ No. 　　沒有。

⑦ Is this allowed on the plane? 　　這可以帶上飛機嗎？

⑧ What time will we be boarding? 　　我們什麼時候登機？

⑨ Where is the departure gate? 　　登機門在哪裡？

⑩ I'm here on vacation. 　　我是來度假的。

取自 YouTube
機場篇

071

機場櫃檯
Checking in at the Airport

ground staff (n.) 地勤人員

I missed my flight because I fell in love with the **ground staff** and refused to leave her. I was later taken away by security.

我錯過了我的班機,因為我愛上了幫我處理票務的地勤,所以不願意離開。我後來被警衛帶走了。

check (v.) 托運

I'd like to **check** this Hello Kitty luggage case. I know I'm a grown man. Don't judge me for my taste.

我的凱蒂貓行李箱要托運。我是成年男子沒錯,不要取笑我的喜好。

aisle seat (n.) 靠走道的位子

When I get an **aisle seat**, I like to make it hard for people to cross and watch them struggle.

我坐在走道座位時會故意讓人很難通過,然後看他們掙扎。

boarding pass (n.) 登機證

I've booked you a flight to "Far Away From Me". Here's your **boarding pass**.

我幫你訂了機票到「離我遠一點」,這是你的登機證。

Ground Staff 地勤 Ray 阿滴

072

 Where are you flying to today? | 請問今天要飛往哪裡？

 Boston. Here's my passport. | 波士頓，這是我的護照。

 Good evening, Mr. Du. Are you **checking** any bags? | 都先生，晚安，有行李要托運的嗎？

 Yes, just one. And I'd prefer an **aisle seat**, please. You know, long flight, gotta get up and stretch. | 有一件，然後我想要靠走道的座位。你知道的，飛很久，要起來走一走。

 No problem. Can you put your luggage on the scale, please? | 沒問題，麻煩您把行李放到上面秤重。

 Of course. It's not overweight, right? | 好的，沒有超重吧？

 Yup, you're good. Here's your **boarding pass**. Your flight leaves from gate 23 and boarding begins at 10:30. | 沒有，這邊是您的登機證。請在 23 號門登機，登機時間是十點三十分。

 Thank you. Also, can I bring my water bottle with me? | 謝謝你，對了，我可以帶水壺嗎？

 Liquids exceeding 100 ml are not allowed through the security checkpoint. You might have to empty your bottle. | 超過一百毫升的液體無法通過安檢，可能得麻煩您清空瓶子。

 Thanks for the reminder! | 謝謝提醒！

Vocabulary
主題單字

Airport Facilities 機場設施

information desk
詢問處

lost and found
失物招領

baggage claim
行李提領區

currency exchange
外幣兌換

coin locker
投幣式置物櫃

duty free shop
免稅商店

GLOBAL TAX FREE

tax refund
退稅

observation deck
觀景台

check-in counter
報到櫃檯

customs
海關

departures
離境

B1　B1

boarding gate
登機門

arrivals
入境

lounge
候機室

terminal
航廈

過海關
At Immigrations

purpose of visit (n.) 拜訪目的

I don't know why I got deported. All I said was, "My **purpose of visit** is 'going to comic-con and marrying my anime senpai'".

我不知道為什麼我被遣返回國。被問到「拜訪目的」時,我只是說「參加動漫大會跟我的動漫學長結婚」。

go on vacation (phr.) 去度假

Hi, this is just a kind reminder that I'm **going on vacation** and you're not.

嗨,想提醒你一下,我就要去度假了,但是你沒有休假。

profession (n.) 職業;專業

Payday is that one day every month that reminds me I've chosen the wrong **profession**.

每個月的發薪日都會提醒我,我真的選錯職業了。

scanner (n.) 掃描器

Come to think of it, your iPhone home button is like a mini fingerprint **scanner**!

仔細想想,你的 iPhone 按鈕就像是一個迷你指紋掃描器耶!

Customs Officer 海關　 Ray 阿滴

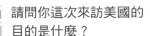
075

 What's the **purpose of your visit** in the United States? | 請問你這次來訪美國的目的是什麼？

 I'm here **on vacation**. | 我是來度假的。

 And how long will you be staying in the States? | 請問，你會在美國停留多久？

 About 15 days. | 大概十五天。

 What's your **profession**? | 你的職業是？

 I'm a YouTuber. | 我是 YouTuber。

 And what's that? | 那是什麼？

 I make videos online and make money off ad revenue. | 我拍影片上傳到網路，然後用廣告分潤賺錢。

 Please look at the camera. Place your fingers on the **scanner**. Now the other hand. Alright, you're good to go. Welcome to the United States. | 請看著攝影機，把手指放到掃描器上。換手。好，可以離開了。歡迎來到美國。

Cultural Notes

出國的時候，過海關（customs）難免會感到緊張；去到入境審核（immigration）較森嚴的國家，更是怕自己不小心漏掉了什麼。首先，要記得填妥海關申報單，以及將所有相關的文件備妥放在身上，千萬不要把重要文件放在行李箱托運！少了這些文件，很有可能就沒辦法順利過海關入境。

租車
Renting a Car

rent (v.) 租用

It's cheap and convenient to **rent** a car from us. You only need to fill out these 24 forms.

跟我們租車很便宜又方便，你只需要填完這 24 張表單就好。

option (n.) 選項

You need to make a choice between Ray and Crown. And not choosing is not an **option**.

阿滴跟滴妹你一定要選一個，然後沒有「不選」這個選項。

insurance (n.) 保險

I hope I get sick constantly this year to make all the money I spent on health **insurance** worthwhile.

希望我今年可以大病特病，我花在健保的錢才值得。

coverage (n.) 覆蓋範圍

The new insurance policy does not include full **coverage** and it costs two times more.

新的保險規定並不包含全保而且還貴兩倍。

Receptionist 接待　 Ray 阿滴

077

 How can I help you today? | 請問今天需要什麼樣的服務呢？

 I would like to rent a car. | 我想要租車。

 We still have some cars available. What kind of car are you looking for? | 我們目前還有一些空車，請問先生想找什麼樣的車呢？

 What are my options? | 有哪些選擇？

 A compact car, a standard car, and a minivan. | 小型車、標準型和小型貨車。

 I'll take the compact car. | 我要小型車。

 How long will you be renting the car? | 請問要租多久呢？

 For one week. | 一個禮拜。

 Do you want to include insurance? We provide full coverage for $12 a day. | 請問要包含保險嗎？全包的話是一天十二塊錢。

 Yes, please. | 好的。

 Can I see your driver's license and a credit card? | 麻煩請您出示駕照和信用卡。

 Here you go. | 這邊。

 Great, now you'll just need to fill out these forms and you can pick up your car downstairs. | 好的，那您填寫完這邊的表格後就可以到樓下取車了。

Vocabulary
主題單字

Rental Car Classes 各種租車

economy
經濟型

compact
小型車；迷你車

intermediate
中型轎車

standard
標準型轎車

full-size
全尺寸

luxury
豪華房車

premium
精選房車

minivan
小型貨車

van
廂型車

pick up truck
貨卡

jeep
吉普車

SUV
(sports utility vehicle)
休旅車

convertible
敞篷車

sports car
跑車

limo (limousine)
豪華禮車

買車票
Getting Train Tickets

one-way (adj.) 單程的

To show how much I appreciate your work here, here's a **one-way** ticket to a deserted island.

為了讓你知道我多重視你，這個去荒島的單程票就給你吧。

round trip (n.) 來回旅行

My **round trip** to the US made me so jet-lagged that I became a morning person. It's a miracle.

我從美國回來後，時差嚴重到我開始每天早起，真是奇蹟。

transfer (v.) & (n.) 轉乘

I was supposed to **transfer** to another train here, but I overslept.

我本來是要在這裡轉另外一班火車的，但我睡過頭了。

direct (adj.) 直達的；直接的

Direct flights are too expensive and connecting flights take too long. Let's just stay home and save us the trouble.

直飛太貴，轉機太久。我們就宅在家裡別出門好了。

Hi, we're trying to get to Boston. Which train should I take?

你好，我們想去波士頓，請問要搭哪班火車？

 Is that **one-way** or **round trip**?

請問單程還是來回票？

 One-way. We're only stopping by.

單程，我們只是路過。

 You can take the 2680 Amtrak train at 4 p.m.

你們可以搭四點的 2680 車次。

 Do we need to **transfer** trains?

需要轉車嗎？

 No, it's a **direct** connection.

不用，那班是直達車。

 How much for 2 adults?

兩個大人多少錢？

 That'll be $30 for 2 regular tickets.

全票兩張是三十元。

 Here you go. Thanks for your help!

這邊，謝謝你的幫忙！

 Yay, tickets. Let me see which platform we should head to...

耶～買到票惹～我看看我們要去哪個月台搭車…

05 { 月台在哪裡

Where's the Right Platform?

platform (n.) 月台

I'm not kidding. I ran into a post in Taipei Main Station and discovered **Platform** 9¾.

沒開玩笑，我撞到台北車站的某根柱子，結果就發現了九又四分之三月台。

underpass (n.) 地下道

Walking in the **underpass** alone at night reminds me so much of horror movies that I usually scream my way out.

晚上獨自走在地下道實在太像恐怖片的場景，我常常尖叫跑出去。

opposite (adj.) 相反的

Do you know what's the **opposite** of "fun"? You.

你知道「好玩」的反義詞是什麼嗎？ 94 你。

sense of direction (n.) 方向感

My **sense of direction** is so bad, even Google Maps gave up on me.

我的方向感差到 Google 地圖也幫不了我。

Are you sure we're on the right platform? | 你確定我們走對月台了嗎？

 To be honest, no. | 老實說，我不確定。

 Our train arrives in 10 minutes! We need to make sure. | 我們十分鐘後就要搭車了欸，我們得確定啊！

 Maybe we can ask that guy in a uniform. | 我們去問那個穿制服的人好了。

 Excuse me, we're trying to get to Boston. Is this the right platform? | 不好意思，我們要去波士頓，這裡是對的月台嗎？

 You guys are on the wrong side. Take the underpass over to the opposite platform. | 你們走錯邊了，走地下道到對面的月台去。

 Got it! Thanks. | 知道了，謝謝！

 I don't understand train stations here. It's so complicated. | 我不懂這裡的車站，好複雜。

 I don't understand your sense of direction. It's so non-existent. | 我不懂你的方向感，你有嗎？

Vocabulary
主題單字

ticket machine
售票機

ticket office
售票口

timetable
時刻表

entrance
剪票口

waiting room
候車室

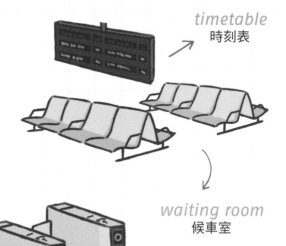

platform
月台

train tracks
軌道

drop off point
下車處

terminal
終點站

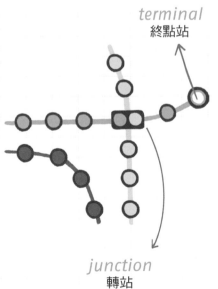

junction
轉站

post box
郵箱

06

叫計程車
Getting a Cab

arrive (v.) 到達

Remember, it's always better to **arrive** late than never.
記得，遲到總比沒到好。

step on it (phr.) 趕快

Step on it! I'm late for Ray's book-signing event!
開快一點！阿滴的簽書會就要開始了！

in a rush (phr.) 急忙地

I play the *Mission Impossible* theme song on speaker when I'm **in a rush** so that people don't get in my way.
每當我很趕的時候，都會用擴音播《不可能的任務》主題曲，就不會有人敢擋我了。

detour (n.) 繞路

I "accidentally" made a **detour** to the bar on my way to church.
我在去教會的路上「不小心」繞路去了酒吧。

Crown 滴妹　 Operator 總機　 Driver 司機　 085

 Could you send a taxi to Boston Park Plaza, please? | 可以派車到波士頓公園廣場酒店嗎？

 Your taxi will arrive in five minutes. | 您的車會在五分鐘內抵達。

(on the taxi) | （計程車上）

 Hi, could you take me to the Children's Museum, please? | 你好，可以載我到兒童博物館嗎？謝謝。

 No problem, are you going to an exhibition? | 沒問題，你是要去看展覽嗎？

 No, I'm just meeting a friend. Um, can you step on it? I'm in a bit of a rush. | 不是，我去找朋友。可以開快一點嗎？我有點趕時間。

 Well, hate to break it to you, but we're in the middle of a traffic jam. | 不好意思，但我們卡在車陣當中。

 Can you take a detour to avoid that? | 你可以繞路避開嗎？

 Nope, I guess you're stuck chatting with me. | 沒辦法，所以你只能繼續跟我聊天了。

Extras

我們有做過【10 個常用的英文句子：計程車篇】，裡面有教十句搭計程車會用到的句子，快掃 QR code 去看看吧！

租腳踏車
Renting a Bike

rental station (n.) 租車站

You're like a **rental station**. Always there when I don't need it; always not when I do.

你就像是租車站一樣。每次不需要時到處都是，需要的時候又都找不到。

block (n.) 街區

I moved into this building because Jay Chou lives just a couple **blocks** away.

我搬進這棟房子主要是因為杰倫就住在附近。

short-term (adj.) 短期的

My **short-term** memory is really bad. On top of that, so is my short-term memory.

我的短期記憶差到講一半會忘記前面講了什麼。

dock (n.) 底座

Putting the bicycle into its **dock** in your first try is like putting a camel through the eye of a needle.

一次就把腳踏車完美歸位到底座上，就像是拿駱駝穿過針眼。

Crown 滴妹 Jane 珍 Guy 路人

087

 Do you know where I can rent a bike in the city?

你知道城裡哪裡可以租腳踏車嗎？

 Beats me. But I do remember seeing a bike **rental station** somewhere.

考倒我了，但我記得在某個地方看到腳踏車租借站。

 There's a guy with one of those bikes right there!

那邊那個男的騎的是那種租的腳踏車欸！

 (Crown walks up.)

（滴妹走上前。）

 Hi there, may I ask where you got the bike from?

你好，可以請問你的腳踏車是在哪租的嗎？

 Oh, it's from the station on Washington Street. A couple of **blocks** that way.

哦！是在華盛頓街的租借站，往那個方向過幾條街就看到了。

 Nice! Can I still get a bike if I don't have a member card?

讚哦！那沒有會員卡可以借車嗎？

 I'm sure you can get a **short-term** pass through their app. If you're planning to do a single ride up to 30 minutes, it's $3 a trip.

你應該可以用它們的 APP 申請短期的證，如果單程超過三十分鐘的話，一趟是三塊錢。

 Wow, that's informative. Thanks!

好詳細的解說，謝謝！

 One last thing, remember to properly lock the bike back into its **dock** when you're returning the bike!

噢，對了，記得還車的時候要把車子鎖回停車架上。

 Are you working for the bike rental program or what? You sure have a lot to say.

你是在租車站工作嗎？你真的介紹得很詳細欸。

119

08

各種轉乘
Transferring at the Station

pick up (phr.) 接（某人）

The app said the driver will **pick** me **up** in 5 minutes. It's been an hour.

APP 說司機五分鐘內會來接我，現在已經過一個小時了。

public transportation (n.) 公共運輸

Looking innocent after farting on **public transportation** is an art.

偷偷在公共運輸上放屁後裝一臉無辜是一門藝術。

shuttle (n.) 接駁車

After an hour sitting beside a crying baby on the **shuttle**, I decided not to have children in the future.

在接駁車上坐在哭鬧的嬰兒旁邊一小時後，我決定以後不生小孩。

terminal station (n.) 終點站

I wonder what will happen if you stay on the MRT after it reaches the **terminal station**.

不知道在捷運抵達終點站之後，繼續待在車廂上會發生什麼事。

Ray 阿滴 Joe 喬

089

 Hey, Joe! I just got off the flight. Where are you? | 嘿，喬，我剛下飛機。你在哪裡？

 Oh man, sorry! Something came up last minute. I'm afraid I won't be able to **pick you up** from the airport. | 抱歉啊兄弟，臨時有點事，我可能不能去機場接你了。

 What? How am I supposed to get to the retreat now? | 什麼？那我要怎麼去度假村啊？

 Relax! It's easy. You just need to take a couple of different **public transportation**. First, you should take the free airport **shuttle** to Boston's South Station, and you get off to transfer to the subway. The subway map is a bit confusing, but just remember you need to get to the **terminal station**, which is Alewife. After you get there, you only have one final transfer to make… | 安啦，很簡單的。你只需要搭幾個不一樣的交通工具就好。首先你要搭免費機場接駁車到波士頓南站，下車後轉捷運。捷運圖有點難懂，但記得你要坐到終點站：埃爾維夫站。到了之後只要再轉乘一次…

 Joe. Come pick me up at the airport. I'll give you $50. | 喬，來機場載我，我給你五十塊。

 On my way. | 我馬上出門。

121

Vocabulary
主題單字

Public Transportation 大眾運輸工具

taxi
計程車

bus
公車

double-decker
雙層巴士

coach
客運

ferry
渡輪

cruise
郵輪

high-speed rail
高鐵

subway / metro
地鐵

tram
有軌電車

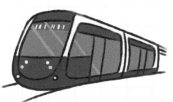

light rail
輕軌車

cable car
纜車

gondola
空中纜車

airplane
飛機

加油站
At the Gas Station

gas station (n.) 加油站

The next **gas station** is all the way through a desert. We're screwed.

下一個加油站要穿過一個沙漠才有。我們完蛋了。

tank (n.) 貯油槽

We need to fill up our **tank** before we set off for our road trip.

出發公路旅行前，我們得先把油箱加滿。

out of order (phr.) 發生故障

I'm just going to put an **"out of order"** sticker on my forehead and call it a day.

我要在我額頭上貼「故障」貼紙，然後就下班。

nozzle (n.) 噴嘴

I am not a man of detail; for example, I often drive away with the **nozzle** still in the car.

我是個不拘小節的人。比如說，我常常會忘記拔油槍就開車走人。

Crown 滴妹 Ray 阿滴

092

 We're almost out of gas. 　我們快沒油了。

 I think there's a **gas station** down the road. Let's fill up our **tank**. 　我記得前面有加油站，我們去加個油吧。

(Ray and Crown arrive at the gas station.) 　（兩人抵達加油站。）

 Wait. This pump says "**out of order**". Let me pull up to the next one. 　等等，這個油槽暫停服務，我開到下一個去。

 These are all self-service pumps. Which type of gas should we get? 　這些都是自助式的油槽，我們要加哪種油？

 I think our car needs unleaded gas, so this button right here. 　應該是加無鉛汽油，按這邊這個按鈕。

 You'll have to pay first for the **nozzle** to be released. 　你得先付錢才能拿油槍。

 Okay. Fair enough. 　喔，對齁。

 We're all set. Full speed ahead! 　加好啦！那我們出發吧！衝啊！

文中用了片語 out of order 來表示機器故障，代表相同意思的片語還有 out of service。通常店家不會完整寫出 The machine is broken. 告知顧客，所以當你看到 out of order 或是 out of service，就代表那個東西目前故障，不提供使用。

125

搭乘公車
Taking a Bus

---

traffic (n.) 塞車；交通流量

Crown's concert tonight caused **traffic** in Taipei.
滴妹今晚的演唱會造成了台北大塞車。

---

give or take (phr.) 大概

Ray: I'll be there in 10 minutes, **give or take**.
我十分鐘後到，大概。

Crown: You always say that before arriving an hour late.
你每次遲到一個小時前都這樣說。

---

catch a ride (phr.) 搭車

Every time I'm trying to **catch a ride** on a bus, the driver speeds away *Fast & Furious* style.
當我每次想趕公車的時候，司機就會快速飆走。

---

crowded (adj.) 擁擠的

I'm most thankful for my height when I'm on a **crowded** bus.
我在人擠人的公車上都會很慶幸我長得高。

Crown 滴妹　 Passenger 乘客

 This bus goes all the way to Mountainview, right?

這台公車會直達山景城嗎？

 Yeah, I suppose.

應該吧。

 How long will it take?

你知道要坐多久嗎？

 Depends on the **traffic**. I'd say an hour, **give or take**.

看交通狀況吧，我想大概是一個小時左右。

 Great, that means I'll be on time for the event. If I hadn't caught this bus, I never would have made it.

太好了，這表示我趕得上活動。要是沒搭是這班車，我應該會遲到。

 Mmm hmm...

嗯嗯…

 Do you ride this bus often? It's so **crowded**!

你常搭這班車嗎？超擠的欸！

 Not really. I usually drive.

沒有，我開車居多。

 So why aren't you driving?

那你今天怎麼沒開車？

 To get some rest on the way. By the way, that was a hint for you to stop talking to me.

我想休息一下，意思就是，你不要再跟我講話了。

11 〔 我迷路了 〕
I Lost My Way

intersection (n.) 十字路口

Traffic lights are extra confusing at **intersections**. It's like I never know when to cross.

十字路口的紅綠燈超難懂，我根本不知道什麼時候可以過。

head down (phr.) 往、去

When I said **head down** Roosevelt Rd., I don't mean keep your head down all the way there.

我說往羅斯福路走，不是叫你在路上邊走邊低著頭。

street (n.) 街

I might seem like a lady on the **street**, but just take me to a buffet restaurant and I'll blow your mind.

我可能在街上看起來是個淑女，但是你帶我去吃吃到飽就會大開眼界。

lane (n.) 巷弄　　　**road** (n.) 路

alley (n.) 小巷　　　**avenue** (n.) 大道

boulevard (n.) 大道

Ray 阿滴   Passerby 路人

 I'm sorry. Could you tell me where the nearest subway station is?

不好意思，請問最近的捷運站是哪裡？

 Yes, it's that way. Head down Palmer **Street** and turn left at the **intersection**. It's on the corner, across from a gift shop.

哦！在那個方向，沿著帕瑪街走，然後交叉路口左轉。就在轉角，禮品店的對面。

 Which intersection do you mean?

請問你指的是哪個交叉入口？

 Just the first one you see. I think it's Palmer Street and King's **Avenue**.

你看到的第一個就是了，我記得是帕瑪街跟國王大道的交叉口。

 Just to double check. **Head down** Palmer Street, and turn left at the intersection?

再確定一次，沿著帕瑪街走，然後交叉路口左轉，是嗎？

 Yup, you got it.

對，沒錯。

 Thanks, Google Maps. You're the best!

謝謝你，Google 地圖，你最棒了！

 ...

...

Say It Right

路標上的英文有 Ave, Rd, St, Ln, Dr, Way, Pl, Blvd 等等各種標示，但這些到底有什麼差別呢？ Road (Rd) 指的是連接兩個點的道路，並沒有什麼格外的條件。Street (St) 則是指連接建築物的道路，通常是東西向；而 Avenue (Ave) 則是 street 的相反，通常為南北向的道路。Boulevard (Blvd) 指的是兩側或中間有整排路樹的道路，像是椰林大道。Lane (Ln) 則是狹窄的道路，通常沒有安全島。Drive (Dr) 屬私人且蜿蜒的道路，Way 則是脫離大路的小路。

警察先生幫幫我
Help Me! Officer!

---

describe (v.) 描述

It's really hard to **describe** you in one word. I can think of 10 insults right off the bat.

要用一個字描述你太困難了。我隨便都想得到十個可以拿來罵你的單字。

---

valuable (n.) 珍貴、值錢的物品

Ray: I'm putting my **valuables** into the safe.
　　　我要把我值錢的東西放進保險櫃。

Crown: That's an Elmo pencil box.
　　　　那是一個 Elmo 鉛筆盒。

---

file (v.) 提出

I'll **file** a report for you even though it seems pointless.

就算看起來沒什麼意義，但我還是會幫你報案。

---

police report (n.) 警方報告

Humor is when you get robbed of your wallet and have to pay $5 for the **police report**.

當你錢包被搶了，還得付五塊錢做警方報告，真的很幽默。

Crown 滴妹　　 Police 警察

098

 Excuse me, officer. I lost my wallet!

不好意思，警察先生，我把皮夾弄丟了！

 Do you remember when and where you lost it?

你記得是什麼時候、在哪裡弄丟的嗎？

 It was in my purse when I left my hotel this morning! I took the subway to Central Park and when I was about to pay for some snacks, I couldn't find it in my purse!

我早上離開飯店的時候，皮夾還在包包裡！然後我搭了地鐵到中央公園，準備要買些點心的時候，就找不到了！

 Okay, miss. Calm down. We're here to help you. Can you describe what your wallet looks like and the valuables it contains?

好的，小姐你先冷靜，我們會幫你。可以形容皮夾的外形和裡面有什麼貴重物品嗎？

 It's a long black wallet with a *One Piece* key chain on it. I have my ID card, 2 credit cards, and about $200 worth of cash in it.

是一個黑色長夾，上面有個海賊王的鑰匙圈。裡面有我的身份證，兩張信用卡和大概兩百多塊的美金現金。

 I'll file a police report to establish a record of your loss. And I would recommend that you call the credit card company to cancel your credit cards just in case.

我會幫你報案然後開立遺失證明，以防萬一，我建議你先打給信用卡公司取消你的信用卡。

 Thanks for the help, officer. I'll see if I can find it on my way back. And please do contact me if you have information on where it might be.

謝謝你的幫忙，我會看看回去的路上會再找一找。如果有任何消息，麻煩你一定要通知我！

 Will do, miss.

沒問題。

131

暖身　十句常用校園英文

① **Can I borrow your pen?**　可以跟你借筆嗎？

② **May I use the restroom?**　可以去廁所嗎？

③ **Use your head!**　用點腦！

④ **Leave me alone!**　不要煩我！

⑤ **Beats me.**　考倒我了。

⑥ **Do we have any homework?**　我們有作業嗎？

⑦ **Hang in there.**　加油／撐著點。

⑧ **There's a test tomorrow?**　明天有考試哦？

⑨ **What was that again?**　剛剛說啥？

⑩ **Oh, crap!**　糟了！

取自 YouTube
校園篇

01

室友日常
Life with Roomie

take out (phr.) 將⋯拿出去

Joe: I **took out** the trash because it was beginning to smell.
我把垃圾拿出去，因為它已經開始發臭了。

Ray: Don't tell me you threw away my stinky tofu.
你該不會把我的臭豆腐丟了吧。

do the dishes (phr.) 洗碗

I want to marry the prince so that I don't have to worry about **doing the dishes** for the rest of my life.
我想嫁給王子，因為這樣我下半輩子就不用擔心要洗碗了。

common room (n.) 交誼廳

Nothing lights up the **common room** like your absence.
當你不在時，交誼廳整個都變舒服了。

afford (v.) 負擔得起

Are you sure you want to have dinner at this restaurant? I don't think you can **afford** it.
你確定要在這間餐廳吃晚餐？我覺得你可能付不起。

Ray 阿滴 Joe 喬

100

 Joe, for the last time, you need to **take out** the trash after dinner.

喬，講最後一次，吃完晚餐要倒垃圾。

 I'll do that after I finish this banana.

我吃完這根香蕉後就去倒。

 And what did I say about **doing the dishes**?

我是不是說過要洗碗？

 I'm just soaking them in hot soapy water. I'll get to them.

我只是先把它們泡在熱肥皂水裡，我等下會洗啦！

 You're just going to leave it there forever.

你只會一直把碗放在水槽裡。

 Hey, there's a welcome party at the **common room** tonight, wanna go?

欸，今天晚上交誼廳有派對欸，要去嗎？

 No, I've got homework to do.

不要，我要寫作業。

 Cool story, bro.

好喔。

 Don't try to change the subject! I'm seriously thinking about kicking you out of my room.

不要轉移話題！我真的考慮把你踢出房間哦！

 Don't even think about it. You can't **afford** the rent without me.

別傻了，沒有我你連房租都付不起。

Cultural Notes

國外宿舍房間通常會有小廚房給學生開伙。入宿說明會時會特別跟學生說明煮飯時開抽油煙機的重要性；這是因為房間裡的煙霧偵測較為敏感，若沒有開抽油煙機的話，很容易被誤以為是房間失火。

Facilities in Dorms 常見宿舍設施

recreation room
娛樂室

study lounge
閱讀室

laundry room
洗衣房

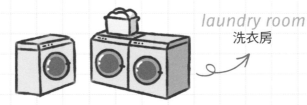

fitness center
健身中心

common room
交誼廳

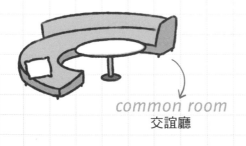

bedding
床包

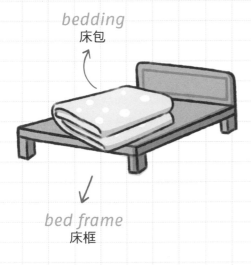

bed frame
床框

mailbox
信箱

fire alarm
火警警報器

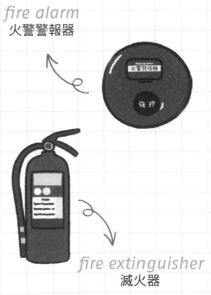

fire extinguisher
滅火器

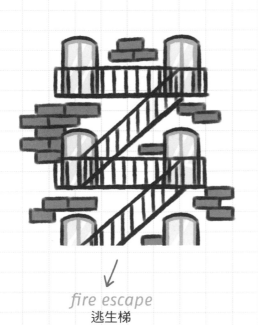

fire escape
逃生梯

跟教授開會
Meeting with the Professor

go over (phr.) 查看

Let's quickly **go over** our finances to make sure we don't have enough budget for the year-end bonus.

我們快速看一下財務報表來確保今年沒辦法發年終。

discuss (v.) 討論

Best friends **discuss** poop.

最好的朋友會討論彼此的排便狀況。

thesis (n.) 論點

My **thesis** has been rejected by the professor for the fifth time. I don't know what's wrong.

我的論點被教授退件第五次了，我不知道哪裡出了差錯。

presentation (n.) 簡報

He did a **presentation** on "How to Be a YouTuber", but only has 10 subscribers himself.

他做了一個「如何當 YouTuber」的報告，但他自己只有 10 個訂閱者。

Come in.

請進。

 Good afternoon, professor. I made an appointment with you at four.

教授，午安。我跟您約了四點要開會。

 Yes, please have a seat. I'd like to **go over** your research paper outline with you. Did you print out the files I sent you yesterday?

對，請坐。我想跟你討論你的論文大綱，你有把我昨天寄給你的檔案印出來嗎？

 Yes, I have them right here. Is the overall structure of my essay okay?

有，都在這，請問我的架構大致上還可以嗎？

 I marked up all the changes you should make, but I'd also like to **discuss** the direction of your essay. Do you have any idea so far?

我把所有要改的地方都標起來了，但我也想跟你討論文章方向，你目前有什麼想法嗎？

 I came up with a few ways to elaborate on my **thesis**, but I haven't finished reading the sources, so I'll probably decide after I do so.

我想了幾個延伸我的主題的方式，但我還沒有讀完資料，所以想等讀完後再決定。

 Sounds like a plan. But I would like to see a more precise direction in your **presentation** next class.

聽起來是個不錯的點子，但下個禮拜課堂的報告上我想看到更明確的方向。

Okay, I'll work on it. Thanks for your time!

我會努力的，謝謝教授！

03 聊課外活動
Extracurricular Activities

pamphlet (n.) 小冊子

Ray: No one reads the **pamphlets** in the box.
沒有人會讀盒子裡的小冊子好嗎？

Crown: No wonder you can't put the chair together.
難怪你沒辦法把椅子裝好。

club (n.) 社團

I don't want to join any **clubs** because I am a loner.
我不想加入任何社團，因為我很邊緣。

extracurricular activity (n.) 課外活動

My favorite **extracurricular activity** is going back home after school and take really long naps until it's dinner.
我最喜歡的課外活動就是下課回家，然後睡午覺睡到要吃晚餐為止。

recreational (adj.) 消遣娛樂的

I used to think that volleyball was just **recreational**, until I watched 3 seasons of *Haikyuu*.
我原本認為排球只是消遣娛樂，直到我追完三季的《排球少年》。

Crown 滴妹  Jane 珍

 I got this **pamphlet** from the club exhibition last week.

我上個禮拜在社團博覽會拿到了這個手冊。

 You're thinking about joining a **club**?

你在考慮加入社團嗎？

 Not really, I'm thinking about participating in **extracurricular activities**.

不算是耶，我想參加一些課外活動。

 I've recently just started an internship and I think it's super helpful for future career prospects.

我最近開始實習，我覺得對職涯準備來說滿有幫助的。

 Well, that's a bit too serious. I want something **recreational**.

實習感覺有點太嚴肅，我想找些休閒性質的。

 How about the photography club? I heard they go on trips on weekends and take photos everywhere they go.

攝影社怎麼樣？我聽說他們週末都會出去玩，然後到哪裡都在拍照。

 That sounds so tiring though!

聽起來很累耶！

 Alright, then maybe the chess club. You won't have to move around as much.

好啦，不然西洋棋社呢。你就不用動來動去了。

 Making decisions is so hard. I feel like taking a nap.

做決定好難，我想要睡午覺了。

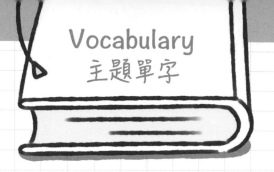

Vocabulary
主題單字

Clubs in College 大學社團

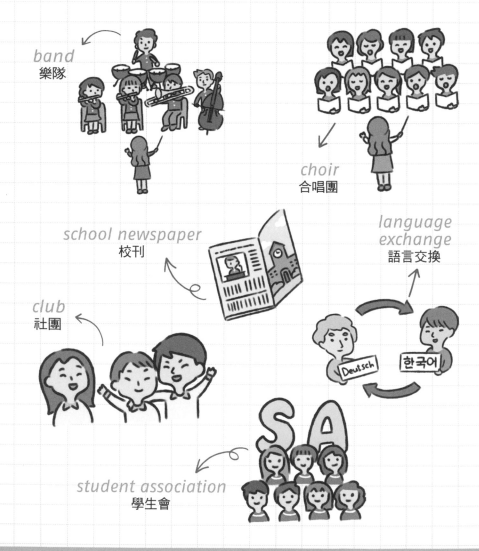

band
樂隊

choir
合唱團

school newspaper
校刊

language exchange
語言交換

club
社團

student association
學生會

varsity
校隊

cheerleading
啦啦隊

volunteer
志工

part-time job
打工

internship
實習

fraternity
兄弟會

sorority
姊妹會

跟同學借筆記
Can I Borrow Your Notes?

---

borrow (v.) 借入

Can I borrow some money from you and never return it?
我可以跟你借一些錢然後永遠不還嗎？

---

anxious (adj.) 焦慮的

The sound of fingernails scraping on chalkboard makes me anxious.
指甲刮黑板的聲音讓我很焦慮。

---

credit (n.) 學分

Ray: **Please, Professor. I need these three credits to graduate.**
拜託啦教授，我需要這三學分才能畢業。

Professor: **You shall not pass.**
我不會讓你過的。

---

take notes (phr.) 做筆記

You might think that your students are taking notes, but more often than not, they are just scribbling.
你可能會以為學生在做筆記，但是其實他們都只是在塗鴉。

Ray 阿滴 Joe 喬

108

 You're early today.

你今天好早到。

 Yeah, can I **borrow** your notes?

嗯啊，可以借我筆記嗎？

 No, you may not.

不行。

 Come on, Ray. I promise it won't happen again.

拜託啦，阿滴。我發誓這是最後一次。

 You've never been so **anxious** about studying. What gives?

你從來都沒因為唸書這麼焦慮，是怎樣？

 I just realize I'm two **credits** away from graduating. And I really need to pass this course!

我發現我差兩學分就可以畢業了，而且我真的必須要過這堂課！

 Well, too bad you never **took notes** in class.

誰叫你上課都不抄筆記。

 Don't be so stingy! I promise I'll start paying attention in class.

不要這麼小氣嘛！我發誓我會開始認真上課！

 Fine, you can have my notes... for 50 bucks.

好啦，我借你筆記…借一次五十塊。

Say It Right

中文裡面，我們會說「寫筆記」或是「做筆記」，但轉換成英文之後，可別說成 write notes 或是 do notes。正確的動詞搭配是 take notes。可是當你想要表達「寫便條給某個人」時，就要寫 write a note to someone，就不是搭配 take 這個動詞了。

145

雷組員
Teammate Slacks Off

blow someone off (phr.) 放鴿子

This is the third time you **blew** me **off** this week, and it's only Wednesday.

這是你這禮拜第三次放我鴿子了，而且才星期三。

slack off (phr.) 偷懶

I'm working really hard to find a job where I can **slack off**.

我非常的努力在找一份可以讓我偷懶的工作。

oversleep (v.) 睡過頭

I hate it when I **oversleep** at work and end up getting home late.

我真心不喜歡上班時貪睡，結果錯過下班時間還晚到家。

contribution (n.) 貢獻

I'd like to thank you for your **contribution** on the project, which is nothing at all.

我想謝謝你對這個企劃的貢獻，也就是什麼貢獻都沒有。

Ray 阿滴　 Jane 珍　 Joe 喬

 I can't believe Joe **blew** us **off**! This is the final presentation!

我不敢相信喬竟然放我們鴿子！這可是期末報告欸！

 I know, right? Not to mention how he's been **slacking off** throughout the discussion. He's the only one that shows up late.

真的！更不用說他討論的時候一直偷懶！只有他每次都遲到。

 Yeah, and this morning, he literally just texted me and said, "**Overslept**."

對！而且今天早上，他只傳簡訊跟我說：「睡過頭。」

 That's it?

就這樣？

 That was all he sent me! He didn't even bother to apologize!

對啊！就這樣！他連道歉都沒說！

 That's it. I'm telling the professor!

我受夠了，我要去跟教授說！

 I'm with you! This is a group project and I refuse to let someone who's made zero **contribution** get the same score as I do.

我跟你一起去！這是團體報告，我絕對不會讓毫無貢獻的人跟我拿一樣的分數！

 Guys, I'm sitting right here.

安安各位，我就坐在這裡耶。

搭訕學妹
Picking up Girls

---

pick up line (n.) 搭訕的話

Use that **pick up line** on me again and I'll punch you in the face.

再把那句搭訕的話用在我身上,我就揍你。

---

give up (phr.) 放棄

Whenever I go on a diet, there's a voice in my head telling me to just **give up**.

每當我要減肥的時候,我的腦海裡都有個小小聲音叫我「放棄吧」。

---

out of someone's league (phr.) 配不上

Not only am I **out of your league**, we're not even playing the same sport.

你不只配不上我,是天差地遠的那種配不上。

---

type (n.) 類型

You're really nice, considerate, reliable, and not my **type**.

你人很好,很貼心,很可靠,很不是我的菜。

Joe 喬　 Ray 阿滴　 Crown 滴妹

112

 Hey, Ray. I'm gonna go over there and ask that girl for her number.

欸阿滴，我要過去跟那個女生要電話。

 Yeah, good luck with that…

呃…祝你好運…

 Hey, it's Angel, right?

嗨，你叫天使對吧？

 Um…no? My name's Crown.

呃…不是，我叫滴妹。

 Funny, because I swear I just saw you fall from the sky.

怎麼會，我發誓我剛看到你從天上掉下來！

 Nice **pick up line**, dude…

啊不就很會撩…

 You think so, too? Do you wanna hang out later? The weather is perfect today!

你也這樣覺得嗎？等下要不要一起出去玩？今天天氣很好欸！

 No, it's too hot outside. I think I'm heading home.

不要，今天太熱了，我要回家。

 I agree. Because to me, you're the perfect weather.

我同意，因為對我來說，你才是最完美的天氣。

 Oh gosh, I can't look at this anymore. Dude, just **give up**. She's **out of your league**.

噢天呀我看不下去了。欸你放棄吧，你高攀不起啦！

 What are you talking about? I'm just getting started.

你在說什麼啊！好戲才正要開始欸！

Extras

我們有做過跟搭訕有關的影片，裡面有教五種用英文「撩人」的方式。快掃 QR code 去看看吧！

149

詢問考試
There's a Test Tomorrow?

midterm (n.) 期中考

I wish my friends would remind me of the **midterm** two weeks in advance, just to give me enough time to procrastinate before I panic.

好希望我的朋友們會在期中考前兩週提醒我，這樣在我慌張之前還有時間可以發懶。

last minute (phr.) 在最後一刻

Sorry, I had to cancel **last minute**. It took me ages to think of an excuse that I've never used before.

對不起我在最後一刻才取消，要想出新藉口真的花了我很多時間。

cram (v.) 死記硬背

My secret tip to getting straight A's is to **cram** as much as you can before the test.

我考高分的秘訣就是考試前死背越多越好。

review (v.) & (n.) 複習

I tried **reviewing** for the midterm, but I ended up falling asleep at my desk.

我試著為期中考複習但最後卻在書桌前睡著。

Oh! We have a test tomorrow? | 噢!明天有考試喔?

 Excuse me, the **midterm**? | 傻眼,期中考啊!

 I need to write that down somewhere. | 我得寫下來。

 Pay attention in class! I feel like a babysitter. | 上課專心好嗎?我很像你的保母欸!

 How many chapters will the exam cover? | 考試要考幾章啊?

 Everything we've covered in class up till now, plus pages 267 to 273. | 目前為止上課有教的地方,外加 267 到 273 頁。

 What! Guess I'll have to do a lot of **last-minute cramming**… | 什麼?天呀我整個臨時抱佛腳欸…

 If you need my notes to help you **review** better… | 如果你需要我的筆記幫你複習的話…

 I'll take them. | 我要!

Too bad. I'm not offering. | 可惜了,我才不給。

Extras

我們有做過做筆記的影片,裡面有教跟如何做筆記相關的撇步和重點,快掃 QR code 去看看吧!

151

聊喜歡的運動
Are You into Sports?

jersey (n.) 運動衫

I had my basketball **jersey** custom-made to show how professional I am.

我的籃球衣是訂做的，讓我看起來專業一點。

junkie (n.) 瘋狂喜愛某事的人

I know it might be hard to believe, but I'm secretly a video game **junkie**.

我知道很難相信，但我私下超愛打電動。

root for (phr.) 支持

Don't ask me who I'm **rooting for** in the election. I don't even know who's running.

不要問我選舉支持誰，我連誰有參選都不知道。

racket (n.) 球拍

Trying out a new **racket** by hitting someone's head with it is a fetish of mine.

我的怪癖是拿到新球拍就打某個人的頭來測試。

Ray 阿滴 Joe 喬

 Nice **jersey**, Joe. What's the occasion? | 喬，運動服很好看哦！要去哪？

 World Cup 2018 kicked off and I'm officially entering full-on football **junkie** mode. | 2018 世界杯足球賽開踢了，我進入超級足球迷模式。

 I didn't know you're into football. Who are you **rooting for**? | 我都不知道你喜歡足球欸，你支持誰啊？

 Argentina all the way, man! Don't you see my blue and white kit? | 無限期支持阿根廷啊！你沒看到我穿藍白球衣嗎？

 Right… I'm not much of a football fan. I like sports that are played with my hands. | 喔是喔，我不是足球迷欸，我比較喜歡用到手的運動。

 Like basketball and volleyball? | 你說像籃球跟排球嗎？

 Not really, more like the ones that require handles. | 不太算，我喜歡會用到把手的。

 You mean… **racket** sports like tennis and badminton? | 哦～你說像網球跟羽球那種有球拍的運動？

 No, it just means I like playing video games because it requires my fingers on the controller at all times. | 不是，我是指我喜歡打電動因為我的手指無時無刻都要在手把上。

153

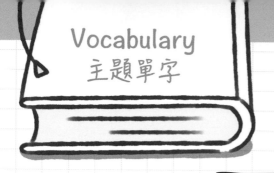

Vocabulary
主題單字

Sports 各種運動

table tennis
桌球

badminton
羽毛球

golf
高爾夫

tennis
網球

volleyball
排球

rugby
橄欖球

American football
美式足球

soccer / football
足球

gymnastics
體操

wrestling
摔角

karate
空手道

basketball
籃球

baseball
棒球

swimming
游泳

cycling
騎單車

archery
射箭

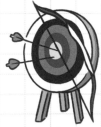

155

翹課人生
Skipping Class

take the roll call (phr.) 點名

Taking the roll call is like a language test, people's names can be so hard to pronounce sometimes.

點名很像語言測驗，有時候有些人的名字真的超難唸。

permission (n.) 許可

My wife is the boss. I've given her **permission** to say so.

我老婆是一家之主，我已經許可她這樣自稱了。

absent (adj.) 缺席的

Sleeping in class is considered being **absent**. So wake up!

課堂上睡覺也算是缺席，所以趕快醒醒！

skip (v.) 不出席

Can I **skip** the part where I have to be a working adult and get right to the part where I retire?

我可以跳過工作階段然後直接到退休生活嗎？

Ray 阿滴　 Joe 喬

 Hey, where do you think you're going?　欸，你要去哪裡？

 What do you mean? The professor already **took the roll call**.　什麼意思？教授點完名了啊。

 And how does that give you **permission** to leave?　這不代表你可以離開了啊。

 Dude, live a little. Once the roll call is taken, it means that I'm not **absent**.　大哥，活在當下好嗎？點完名就代表我有來上課啊。

 I'm going to tell the professor that you're **skipping** class.　我要跟教授說你翹課。

 You wouldn't.　你才不會。

 I sure will. Wanna bet?　我會！要不要賭？

 How about I make you a deal?　不然我們打個商量，好不好？

 What's in it for me?　我有什麼好處？

 I'll buy you lunch for the rest of the week.　我這禮拜請你吃午餐。

Done. Wait, it's already Friday!　成交。欸等下，今天已經禮拜五了欸！

講笑話
Tell Me a Joke

joke (n.) 笑話

The **joke** was so hilarious that I laughed for three days.
那個笑話好笑到我笑了三天。

fire away (phr.) 開始說話

You have exactly 1 minute before I lose my patience.
Fire away!
我只會給你一分鐘的耐心,開始講吧!

pun (n.) 雙關

Understanding the **puns** in jokes is perhaps one of the most difficult things in the world.
理解笑話裡的雙關應該是世界上最難的事情之一。

buzzkill (n.) 掃興

Stop being a **buzzkill**. You're ruining all the fun!
不要再掃興了啦!都被你弄的不好玩了。

Crown 滴妹 Jane 珍

 Hey, Jane, my friend told me a **joke** on the other day, wanna hear it? | 珍，我朋友那天跟我講了個笑話，要不要聽？

 Sure, **fire away**. | 好啊，你說吧！

 A pony goes to the doctor, but he can't speak. So, the doctor examines him and says, "I know what the problem is, you're a little hoarse!" | 有隻小馬沒辦法說話去看醫生。醫生檢查之後說：「我知道問題是什麼了！你有點沙啞。」

 I don't get it. | 我不懂。

 A pony is a little horse. Get it? | 小馬就是很小的馬啊，懂嗎？

 Oh… I always have a hard time getting the **puns**. | 哦…我每次都不懂這些雙關。

 It's okay. Here's another one, "What do snowmen do in their spare time?" | 沒關係，還有一個：「雪人閒暇時在幹嘛？」

 Um… Stay still? | 呃…站著不動？

 Just chilling. | 在旁邊涼快啦！

 I'm probably a **buzzkill**, but how is that funny? | 噢，我真的很煞風景，但這笑點在哪…？

Cultural Notes

　　每當我們要講笑話時，主角不外乎就是「小明」，但其實在英文裡面，也有個很常出現在笑話裡當主角的人，他就是 Little Johnny。在英文裡，Little Johnny Jokes 就是那些以 Little Johnny 這個小男生為主角。

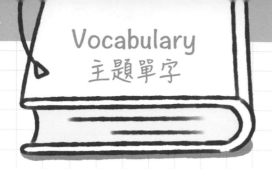

Vocabulary
主題單字

Dad Joke 爸爸笑話

Kid: What do you call a chicken staring at some lettuce?

Dad: Chicken Caesar Salad.

- Instagram

Caesar Salad 音似 sees her salad。

Walks into a Bar Joke 走進酒吧笑話

A guy walks into a bar -- and sustains a mild concussion.

- Comedy Central

walk into 有「走進…」和「撞上…」之意，concussion 則是「腦震盪」。

Little Johnny Joke 小強尼笑話

Teacher: Why are you praying in class, little Johnny?

Little Johnny: My mom taught me to always pray before going to sleep.

- short-funny.com

Blonde Joke 金髮美眉笑話

A: How do you make a blonde's brain the size of a pea?

B: Inflate it.

- Comedy Central

inflate 為「充氣」之意，用來嘲諷金髮美眉原本就沒什麼腦，要讓她的腦變成豌豆大，只要稍微充氣就好。

Knock knock Joke 敲門笑話

A: Knock, knock

B: Who's there?

A: Merry.

B: Merry who?

A: Merry Christmas

- Funology.com

 Merry 和女人名 Mary 同音。

Cross the Road Joke 過馬路笑話

A: Why did the turkey cross the road?

B: Because he wasn't a chicken.

- Comedy Central

 chicken 有「雞」和「膽小鬼」的意思。

午餐吃什麼
What's for Lunch?

famished (adj.) 非常飢餓的

I'm not sure if I'm bored or **famished**. Let's get some ice cream to make sure.

我不太確定我是無聊還是餓。我吃吃看冰淇淋確定一下。

canteen (n.) 餐廳、販賣部

I'm so poor I can't afford anything outside the school **canteen**.

我窮到只買得起學校販賣部的食物。

on campus (phr.) 校園裡

The print shop **on campus** charges way less than the ones off campus.

學校裡的影印店比校外的便宜很多。

joint (n.) 餐館

Sure, I'll meet you guys at the usual **joint.** Just give me an hour or two to ask my girlfriend for permission.

好啊，我們就老地方見。只要給我一兩個小時說服我女友讓我去就好了。

 Crown 滴妹　 Jane 珍

124

 I'm **famished**. What's for lunch?

我要餓死了，中午要吃什麼？

 Um, I don't know. The main **canteen** is down for maintenance. So our only option is the smaller café. Maybe the BBQ rice bowl?

我不知道耶，大食堂在維修，只能去小咖啡廳吃了。要吃燒肉丼飯嗎？

 Nah, we had that two days ago.

不要，兩天前才吃過。

 What about those Mexican wraps? We haven't had that for a while.

還是墨西哥捲餅？有一陣子沒吃了。

 I had diarrhea last time I had that.

我上次吃拉肚子。

 School only started and we're already bored with the all the food options **on campus**.

才剛開學我們就吃膩校園裡的食物了。

 I want pizza and fried chicken! School food sucks!

我要吃披薩跟炸雞啦！學校的食物爛透了！

 Sorry, the nearest pizza **joint** is 10 km from here.

不好意思，最近的披薩店在十公里外。

163

畢業
On Graduation Day

robe (n.) 長袍

Remember to bring your **robe** to graduation. And no, I don't mean the one you bought at the *Harry Potter* Studio Tour.

記得帶你的長袍去畢業典禮，然後不是你在《哈利波特》片場導覽買的那件。

graduation (n.) 畢業典禮

Students should get a bill on their **graduation** to remind them how much it cost.

學生們應該在畢業典禮拿到帳單，提醒他們大學花了多少錢。

cap (n.) 帽子

Ray, how many times do I have to tell you my graduation **cap** is not a cosplay prop?

阿滴，我要跟你說多少次？我的畢業帽不是拿來給 cosplay 的。

valedictorian (n.) 畢業生致詞代表

It takes all sorts to make a world. I was **valedictorian** of my class and my brother missed his graduation.

一樣米養百樣人，我是我們班的畢業生代表，而我哥缺席了他的畢業典禮。

Crown 滴妹　　 Ray 阿滴

 What are you doing in my robe?

你幹嘛穿著我的學士袍？

 It's graduation day. Can you grab me my cap?

今天是畢業典禮啊，可以拿學士帽給我嗎？

 It's MY graduation day, not yours.

今天是「我的」畢業典禮，不是你的。

 No, it's mine. And I have been rehearsing my valedictorian speech for months.

哪有，是我的。我已經演練我的畢業生代表演講好幾個月了。

 Knock it off! You already graduated seven years ago!

不要鬧了！你七年前就畢業了！

 Dear professors and fellow graduates, it is an honor to stand before you...

親愛的教授和畢業生們，今天很榮幸站在台前…

 Stop! And get out of my robe. I'm going to be late for MY graduation. Okay, how about we compromise? I'll exchange the cap for my robe.

夠了！快點脫掉我的學士袍，我快趕不上「我的」畢業典禮了。好，不然我們妥協一下。我用畢業帽跟你換畢業袍。

 I have a terrible sister.

我妹妹真糟糕。

Extras

我們有做過跟畢業有關的影片，裡面有教五種畢業典禮「哭」的方式，還有滴妹當畢業生代表演講的片段哦！快掃 QR code 去看看吧！

暖身 十句常用放假英文

①	Wanna hang out?	要出去玩嗎？
②	What are you up to?	你在幹嘛？
③	No spoilers!	不要爆雷！
④	I'm going on a vacation.	我要去度假。
⑤	Let's just stay in.	我們待在家就好了。
⑥	I'm binge-watching.	我在追劇。
⑦	It's on sale!	大特賣欸！
⑧	Pull an all-nighter.	熬夜。
⑨	I had a blast.	我玩得很開心。
⑩	Time to wake up!	起床！

取自 YouTube
放假篇

01 好想看電影
Wanting to See a Movie

tag along (phr.) 跟隨

I'm heading out, and no, you may not **tag along**.
我要出門了,然後你不可以跟來。

special effects (n.) 特效

Who would have thought Crown was actually made out of **special effects**?
想不到滴妹竟然是電腦特效做出來的。

epic (adj.) 壯麗的

Ray's April Fools' pranks are just **epic**! That's what I tell myself.
阿滴的愚人節惡作劇都超狂的欸!至少我自己是這麼認為的。

sequel (n.) 續集

I hope they make the **sequel** for *Magic Mike* in 3D.
我希望《舞棍俱樂部》的續集是 3D 的。

Joe 喬　 Ray 阿滴

128

 Dude, I'm going to the movies, wanna **tag along**?

欸，我要去看電影，要不要一起來？

 I'm all for it. I've been wanting to see that new Avengers movie since day one!

當然要！我一直都豪～想看新的復仇者聯盟！

 Not again! Why does it always have to be a superhero movie?

又來了！幹嘛每次都要看超級英雄片啊？

 Because the **special effects** are going to be **epic**, what else?

因為特效一定超狂啊，不然勒！

 Not interested.

沒興趣。

 Well, how about the *Jurassic World* **sequel**?

那不然《侏羅紀世界》的續集？

 You can say that again. I already booked the tickets.

很可以！我早就訂好票了。

 For real? Then why did you ask in the first place?

認真嗎？那你剛問心酸的？

169

爆雷啦！
Spoiler Alert!

spoiler (n.) 爆雷

This review contains **spoilers**. Viewer discretion is advised.
這篇評論有雷，請小心服用。

teaser (n.) 前導片

Oh my gosh, BTS just released a **teaser** for their new single!
#ARMY4EVER
我的媽呀，防彈少年團剛出了新單曲的前導影片！
#一日阿米終生阿米

trailer (n.) 預告

An exclusive **trailer** of the final season of *Game of Thrones*! My life is complete!
《權力遊戲》最後一季的的獨家預告！我的人生已無遺憾。

twist (n.) 劇情逆轉

What a **twist**! Ray's sister is fake!
真是太震撼了！滴妹是假的！

Ray 阿滴　 Crown 滴妹

130

 I went and saw *Ready Player One* the other day. Man, it was so good!

欸我那天去看了《一級玩家》，真的 hen 讚～

 Oh yeah? I heard a lot of great things about it.

是嗎？聽說很多人都覺得很好看。

 In the movie, they have to find an Easter egg, and one of the challenges is *The Shining*. I mean, how cool is that?

電影裡面，他們要找彩蛋，其中一個關卡是《鬼店》欸！不覺得超狂的嗎？

 Whoa! What did I say about **spoiler** alerts? I never watch the **teasers** or **trailers** before I see a movie!

欸！我不是說我超討厭爆雷嗎？我都不看前導片或預告的欸！

 Don't be so dramatic. These are all harmless little details.

哪有這麼誇張，這些小細節不算雷吧。

 No way. You'll just ruin the fun! I prefer to enjoy my movies spoiler-free. Thank you.

不不不，這些都是爆雷！我不喜歡沒看電影就被爆雷，謝謝。

 Oh, I haven't told you about the **twist** at the end…

喔，我還沒跟你講最後結局的大逆轉…

 Shut up!!! I'm not listening!

閉嘴！！！我不要聽你說話！

買票看電影
Getting Tickets for a Movie

box office (n.) 售票處;票房

Head over to the **box office** first. I'll park the car and meet up with you.

你先去售票處排隊。我去停車,等等跟你會合。

sold out (phr.) 銷售一空的

Sold out? Ma'am, I'm Ray Du, do you think you can get me a ticket?

賣完了?小姐我是阿滴,你可以幫我生出一張票嗎?

Take it or leave it. 要不要隨便你。

Crown will not be attending the speech, only Ray, **take it or leave it.**

滴妹不會來演講,只有阿滴。要不要參加隨便你。

theater (n.) 影廳

Are you sure we're in the right **theater**? This does not look like *Deadpool*.

你確定我們沒走錯廳嗎?這看起來不像《死侍》。

Ray 阿滴　　 Clerk 售票員

132

 Whew, what's with the line at the **box office** today?

呼，售票亭也排太多人了吧！

 Everyone's here to see the Avengers.

大家都來看復仇者聯盟啊。

 No wonder. Can I get a ticket to see *Avengers: Infinity War* at 3 o'clock, please?

想也知道，那我要一張三點的《復仇者聯盟3：無限之戰》。

 Believe it or not, you got the last ticket and we're all **sold out**.

信不信由你，你買到的是最後一張票。

 No kidding, must be my lucky day. Do I get to choose where I sit?

真的假的？我也太好運了吧！那我可以選位子嗎？

 No. There's only one seat left, **take it or leave it**.

不行啊！只剩一個位子了，不要拉倒。

 Right, sorry. That was a dumb question.

也對，抱歉，我好像問了個蠢問題。

 The movie will be in **theater** 3, that's the second theater on the right.

電影在三廳，右邊的第二間。

Cultural Notes

美國和台灣電影院最大的不同是，並非所有電影院都買票劃位。目前，美國還是有些電影院是買票後自由入座，但有很多人批評這樣的方式，所以有許多電影院已經慢慢在調整，實行買票同時劃位。

去酒吧喝酒
Going to a Bar

shot (n.) 一小口烈酒

You should've never had that second round of **shots**.
你不應該喝第二輪 shots 的。

on the rocks (phr.) 加冰塊

Some people prefer whiskey **on the rocks**, and others straight up.
有些人威士忌喜歡加冰塊，有些人喜歡什麼都不加。

drink until sb. drops (phr.) 喝到掛

She decided it was a good idea to **drink until she drops** on her birthday party.
她覺得在自己的生日派對上喝到掛是個很棒的點子。

hungover (adj.) 宿醉的

I proposed to my boyfriend last night. Now I'm both **hungover** and in regret.
我昨晚跟我男友求婚了。現在我宿醉加上後悔。

Ray 阿滴 Joe 喬

134

 So, this is what a bar looks like. | 原來酒吧長這樣啊…

 Yeah, pretty cool, huh? So what's it gonna be? **Shots**? It's on me. | 對啊，不錯吧！你要喝什麼？ Shot ？我來請客！

 Give me a break. I have to work tomorrow. I'll just have a juice. | 饒了我吧！明天還得上班欸！我喝果汁就好。

 So typical of you. I guess alcohol's just not for you. | 你每次都這樣，還是滴酒不沾啊。

 Whiskey **on the rocks** for you, as usual. Cheers to friendship and happiness. | 你的威士忌加冰塊。敬友誼和快樂。

 Lame. Cheers to **drinking until we drop**! | 噢你也太俗了吧，敬喝到掛啦！

 What? No, you're going to get a **hangover** tomorrow! | 欸不要啦！你明天一定會大宿醉！

Extras

講到 hangover，怎麼能不提《醉後大丈夫》（*Hangover*）這個系列電影呢？這個系列因為初推出太受歡迎，現在已經拍了三集！敘述三個男人每每在參加婚禮前的告別單身派對上豪飲後被下藥，隔天早上醒來所經歷的荒謬事情。面對各種突如其來的震撼，三個大男人能成功脫身，趕到婚禮現場嗎？本片內容被列為輔導級，所以未成年請記得由家長陪同觀賞哦。

Vocabulary
主題單字

Drinks in a Bar 酒吧常見飲料

beer
啤酒

alcohol-free / nonalcoholic
不含酒精

soft drink
軟性飲料

cocktail
調酒

champagne
香檳

wine
葡萄酒

sake
清酒

rum
萊姆酒

whiskey
威士忌

cider
蘋果酒

gin
琴酒

brandy
白蘭地

tequila
龍舌蘭

vodka
伏特加

05 討論喜歡的歌手
Your Favorite Singer

celebrity crush (n.) 偶像

You didn't get this from me, but Crown's **celebrity crush** is Tom Hiddleston.

不要說是我告訴你的，滴妹的偶像是湯姆希德斯頓。

award (n.) 獎項

Best Brother **Award** 2018 goes to Mr. Myself!

2018 最暖哥哥獎的得主是——我本人！

musical artist (n.) 音樂人

The Grammy Award is held annually to celebrate all outstanding **musical artists**.

一年一度的葛萊美獎為所有傑出音樂人喝采。

single (n.) 單曲

Did you download the latest **single** by the internet-famous boy group 'Sweatpant Bois'?

網路天團棉褲男孩的最新單曲你下載了嗎？

Ray 阿滴　 Crown 滴妹

137

 Who's your **celebrity crush**?

你的偶像是誰？

 Hmm… I'll have to say Justin Bieber.

嗯…應該是小賈斯汀吧。

 It's okay. I won't judge.

好的，瞭解。友善尊重包容。

 He's a great singer, okay? He's won countless music **awards** and is one of the best-selling **musical artists** of all time!

他是很棒的歌手，好嗎？他贏了超多個獎項，也製作了很多熱賣的歌曲。

 Well, you don't have to convince me.

你不用說服我啦。

 On top of that, there are 3 number one **singles** on his new album alone!

而且在他最新的專輯裡面，就有三首排行榜第一名的單曲！

 Are you seriously reading off a *Wikipedia* page right now?

你還認真唸維基百科給我聽喔？

Say It Right

　　歌手或歌唱團體發片時，會推出 EP、album 和 single 等形式的作品。但這些到底是什麼意思呢？Single 是所謂的「單曲」，通常只有一到兩首歌，通常包含一首歌的另一種版本（如混音版）。EP (Extended Play) 則是所謂的「短專輯」，介於單曲跟專輯之間，通常有四首歌，總長度在 25 分鐘上下。而 album 就是我們熟悉的「專輯」，架構非常完整，通常超過七首歌，且長度也多於 30 分鐘。

179

去看籃球賽
Going to a Basketball Game

be up against (phr.) 與…競爭

Ray will **be up against** Crown in the running of Favorite YouTuber of the Year.

阿滴跟滴妹將角逐「年度最受喜愛的 YouTuber」。

concession stand (n.) 小吃販賣部

I bet you'll catch Ray at the **concession stand** since he's such a foodie.

既然阿滴這麼愛吃，你應該可以在小吃部遇到他。

half-time (n.) 中場

It's **half-time** now, but you'd better get home fast if you want to catch the third quarter.

現在是中場休息，但你如果要趕上第三節就要快點回家。

commentator (n.) 實況播音員

It's annoying how the **commentator** always gets the players' names wrong.

播報員每次都把球員的名字叫錯，真的很煩。

Ray 阿滴 Joe 喬

139

 So who's playing tonight? | 今天是誰比賽啊？

 It's the first round of the playoffs, and the Warriors **are up against** the Spurs. | 今天是季後賽第一輪，勇士要對上馬刺。

 Okay, I'm going to head over to the **concession stand**. Do you want anything? | 好哦，那我要去販賣部買東西，要幫你買嗎？

 Dude, sit down. The game just started. | 欸坐下啦，比賽才剛開始欸！

 But I really want some popcorn and coke right now. | 但我現在真的很想吃爆米花跟可樂。

 Just wait until **half-time**. Sit down and watch. | 等中場休息啦，坐下看比賽。

 Well, are you going to explain the game to me? | 那你要解釋給我聽嗎？

 What? Just listen to what the **commentator** says and you'll be alright. | 蛤？齁，你聽播報員講就懂了啦！

Cultural Notes

在國外到大型體育館等場所觀看球賽或演唱會，都需要經過安檢（security check），而且安檢規格媲美機場海關，票券上會特別註明不能帶什麼樣的物品入場，以及隨身包包該是什麼樣的大小。為加速安檢速度，很多人會選擇直接把東西放進透明夾鏈袋裡面。輕便的小包包也是比較好的選擇，大背包通常會被禁止帶入場。

討論喜歡的電影
Your Favorite Movie

be into sth. (phr.) 喜歡某件事

I **am** so **into** *Game of Thrones.* I've decided to get myself a pet dragon.
我超迷《權力遊戲》，我決定要養一隻龍。

chick flick (n.) （主打女性觀眾的）愛情電影

Chick flicks are so predictable and filled with cliché.
女生愛看的那種愛情片劇情超好猜又陳腔濫調。

genre (n.) 類別

If I make my life story into a movie, the **genre** will definitely be superhero.
如果把我的人生故事拍成電影，這部片一定是個超級英雄片。

plot (n.) 劇情

The movie adaptation totally messed up the **plot**. Typical.
電影版把劇情搞爛了，真是不意外。

 Jane 珍　Crown 滴妹

 What are you watching, Crown? | 滴妹你在看什麼啊？

 The Notebook. It's such a sad but romantic story. | 《手札情緣》啊，好傷心但好浪漫ＱＱ。

 You're really **into chick flicks**, aren't you? | 你真的很愛浪漫愛情片耶。

 Yeah. Do you want to join me? | 對啊，要不要一起看？

 Ugh, no. Romantic stories make me want to barf. I'm more of an action movie person. Are there any other **genres** you like? | 呃，愛情電影讓我超反胃，我比較喜歡動作片。你有喜歡其他類型的電影嗎？

 Eh, maybe musicals. But it depends on the **plot.** | 可能歌舞片吧，但我滿看劇情的。

 Got it. I'm just going to leave you to it. | 了解，那你繼續看吧。

Say It Right

電影的種類五花八門，但在國外電影頒獎典禮上，並不會依照每個種類頒獎。除了動畫（animated feature）和紀錄片（documentary）是自己單獨的獎項之外，其他的電影都會被用 Picture 來指稱，如最佳影片獎就是 Best Picture。另外，一些電視電影的獎項會將喜劇片（comedy）跟劇情片（drama）分開，所以會有 Best Actor in a Comedy 和 Best Actor in a Drama。

183

Vocabulary
主題單字

Movie Genres 電影類型

action
動作片

comedy
喜劇片

horror
恐怖片

drama
劇情片

adventure
冒險片

animation
動畫片

film noir
黑色電影

musical
歌舞片

142

thriller
驚悚片

*sci-fi
(science fiction)*
科幻片

western
西部片

crime
犯罪片

war
戰爭片

epic
史詩片

biopic
傳記片

documentary
記錄片

08

{ 在遊樂園玩

At the Amusement Park }

attraction (n.) 景點

The restrooms are part of the **attractions** in the park. That's how little we have.

廁所也算是景點之一。可見這個遊樂園有多小。

ride (n.) 遊樂設施

I hate how **rides** are all designed to be seated in pairs. No, it's not because of the fact that I don't have any friends to ride with me.

我很討厭遊樂設施都是要兩個兩個入座的。絕對不是因為我沒朋友所以才討厭。

fastpass (n.) 快速通行證

I secretly love the look of people waiting in line when I use the **fastpass**.

每當我使用快速通行，都愛偷看排隊的人臉上的表情。

parade (n.) 遊行

It took us 20 minutes to realize that we waited at the ending point of a **parade** instead of its starting point.

我們花了二十分鐘才發現，我們守著的地方是遊行的終點而不是起點。

186

Ray 阿滴  Crown 滴妹

144

 Crown, stop taking pictures with the **attractions**. I want to go on all the **rides**!

滴妹你不要再跟景點拍照了！我要去玩遊樂設施啦！

 We still have an hour before we go on the roller coaster. Look at the **fastpass**!

我們還要一個小時才坐得到雲霄飛車，快速通行證上面有寫。

 We can go on other rides for the time being!

這之間我們可以去坐別的啊！

 Okay, just let me take a picture with the mascot.

好啦，我跟吉祥物拍完照就過去。

 Take all the time you need. I'm heading over to the single rider line.

算了你慢慢來，我自己去搭。

 You know what, let's just meet an hour later. I want to check out the **parade**.

一個小時後見算了，我想去看遊行。

 What are you? Three years old?

啥？你三歲小孩嗎？

Cultural Notes

為了紓解人潮，遊樂園在某些設施設有快速通行，但是快速通行一次只能排一個設施，對於想玩到所有設施的人來說，時間會被該設施綁住，反而無法節省時間。這時候，你可以去玩設有所謂 single rider service（單人通行服務）的遊樂設施，如果你是自己一個人，或是不介意跟朋友們分開搭乘的話，就可以利用這個通道！

去聽演唱會
Going to a Concert

tour (v.) & (n.) 巡迴

'Ray is on **tour**. Let's go see him!' said no one ever.

「阿滴在巡迴耶，我們去看看吧！」沒有人這樣說過。

performance (n.) 表演

What do you think of his **performance**? Wait, I know you think it sucks. Me too.

你覺得他的表演如何？等等，我知道你覺得很爛。我也是這麼覺得。

postpone (v.) 延後

I'm so lazy. I even **postpone** procrastination.

我懶到會把拖延症這件事情延後。

refund (v.) & (n.) 退費

The only **refund** I accept is tax refunds.

我能夠接受的退費只有退稅。

Ray 阿滴　Jane 珍

146

 I'm so happy Ed Sheeran's concert **tour** included Taiwan! I listen to his songs all the time.

我超開心紅髮艾德的巡迴演唱會有包含台灣！我常常聽他的歌。

 What? You didn't know? Ed got injured and the whole concert is cancelled.

嗯？你不知道嗎？艾德他受傷了，整個演唱會都取消了。

 You serious? He's got a whole list of countries to go! What about all those **performances**?

你認真？他有超多國家要去耶！那些表演都怎麼辦？

 Well, he announced that most will be cancelled and only a few **postponed**.

他宣布大多數場次都會取消，只有幾個會延期舉辦。

 It's a shame. I was really looking forward to it. I guess I'll just have to ask for a **refund** now.

好可惜喔。我真的蠻期待的說。那現在我只好去辦退票了。

 You haven't applied for a refund? The deadline was yesterday!

你還沒申請退費？昨天截止欸！

 Wonderful. Not only do I not get to see Ed Sheeran, I can't even get my money back.

好喔。我不僅看不到艾德，連錢也拿不回來。

189

Vocabulary
主題單字

Music Genres 音樂類型

alternative
另類音樂

blues
藍調

classical
古典樂

country
鄉村音樂

EDM (electronic dance music)
電子舞曲

funk
放克音樂

folk
民俗音樂

heavy metal
重金屬

hip-hop
嘻哈饒舌

indie
獨立製作

jazz
爵士樂

pop
流行樂

punk
龐克樂

R & B
(rhythm & blues)
節奏藍調

reggae
雷鬼音樂

rock
搖滾樂

宅在家看動漫
Manga and Anime Fanatic

season (n.) 季、季節

My life loses its meaning when I finish every **season** of my favorite anime.

看完每一季喜歡的動畫後，我的人生就失去了意義。

manga (n.) 漫畫

I have the utmost respect for **manga** artists. I bet they never set foot outside of their houses.

我非常敬佩漫畫家，因為他們一定宅得很極致。

release (n.) 連載

When I meet anime fans, I ask them if they follow the manga **release.** If not, I secretly look down on them.

每當遇到動漫迷，我就會問他們有沒有在追連載。如果沒有的話，我會偷偷瞧不起他們。

anime (n.) 動漫

For some reason, whenever I talk about my love for **anime**, girls just stop responding to my texts.

很奇怪，每次我聊到我對動漫的熱愛，女生都會已讀不回。

Ray 阿滴　 Crown 滴妹

149

 Where are you? You should be at the studio by now.

你在哪裡？你現在應該要在工作室了啊。

 I've decided not to head over today. The new _season_ for _Attack on Titan_ has been released.

我今天不過去了。《進擊的巨人》最新一季出了。

 Are you serious? That's my favorite _manga_! I've been following its new _release_ every single month for a year now!

你認真？那是我最愛的漫畫耶！我每個月追連載到現在追了一年了！

 Well, sucks to be you. You still have a whole day of work until you can watch the _anime_.

那真是抱歉囉。你還有一整天的工作要做才能看動漫。

 Wait for me. I'm skipping work and heading home.

等我。我現在馬上翹班回家。

 Screenshot saved. I'm sending this to everyone at work.

截圖。我要把這傳給你公司的同事。

Say It Right

漫畫可以用 comics 或是 manga 來表示，前者源自英文，後者源自日文。不過，
這兩者細分起來其實還是有差別的。manga 通常是以黑白呈現，閱讀時是由
右邊讀到左邊。而 comics 則是彩色呈現，主題多與超級英雄相關，閱讀時則
是由左讀到右。

宅在家打電動
Video Game Junkie

---

expansion (n.) 擴充

We're living in a time where the **expansions** and downloadable contents cost more than the base game.

現在的遊戲，擴充跟可下載的內容加起來比遊戲本身更貴。

---

pre-purchase (v.) & (n.) 預購

Getting people to **pre-purchase** is a scheme created by business profiteers. I'll gladly take it.

開放預購完全是商人的詭計。我全然接受。

---

pay to win (phr.) 付錢就是贏家

I thought only in life, your success will be measured by how rich your dad is. Well, it's the same in **pay-to-win** games.

我以為有個有錢老爸就會成功的事情只發生在現實生活中，但其實在一些付費遊戲裡也是一樣道理。

---

stay in (phr.) 宅在家

Why go hiking when you can **stay in**? I can take little walks indoors as well.

可以宅在家為什麼要去戶外走？我也可以在家裡繞小圈圈。

Crown 滴妹　 Ray 阿滴

151

 Why the grin? You're weirding me out. ｜ 你幹嘛賊兮兮的笑？你很怪。

 The new Hearthstone expansion just came out! I'm so excited about it! I even pre-purchased 70 packs right off the bat. ｜ 最新的爐石擴充上線了！我超興奮，而且一宣佈時我還立馬預購了 70 包卡包。

 Dude, that game is totally pay to win. ｜ 老兄，那個遊戲都是台幣戰士。

 Is not! You need wits and strategy, and of course a lot of packs. ｜ 不是好嗎！你需要智慧跟策略。當然也需要很多卡。

 Which you get by…? ｜ 那卡是怎麼拿到的…？

 Never mind. I don't have time for chit-chat. I'm staying in all day to enjoy busting open new card packs! ｜ 啊隨便啦，我沒時間跟你閒聊。我要整天待在家開我的新卡包。

Extras

我們其實做過滿多跟電玩有關的影片，阿滴為大家整理了一個播放清單，快掃 QR code 去看看吧！

195

Video Game Genres 電玩種類

action-adventure 動作冒險

玩家要找到遊戲過關的關鍵物品之外，還必須通過險峻的地形考驗，或是跟遊戲裡的其他角色進行格鬥。

Ex. 薩爾達傳說 *The Legend of Zelda*

puzzle 益智

益智遊戲著重在「解謎底」，通常需要用各種不同方式解決問題，包含動作、邏輯等等。

Ex. 俄羅斯方塊 *Tetris*

simulation 模擬

這種遊戲模擬現實的環境和事件，讓玩家體驗現實生活中可能發生的情境。此類遊戲通常沒有明顯的結局，多數時候是由玩家決定遊戲走向。

Ex. 模擬市民 *The Sims*

RPG (role-playing) 角色扮演

玩家在虛擬的設定中扮演某個角色，透過遊戲角色與敵人戰鬥來提升等級、收集裝備及完成遊戲設定的任務，藉此體驗劇情的走向。

Ex. 太空戰士 *Final Fantasy*

MOBA (multiplayer-online battle arena) 多人線上戰術擂台

玩家被分為兩隊,每個玩家通常只能控制其中一隊的一個角色,遊戲勝利的條件就是擊敗對方隊伍及其陣地。

Ex. 英雄聯盟 *League of legends*

sports 運動

這種遊戲模擬真實的運動比賽,而內容多以為人所知的大型賽事為腳本。同時,玩家也能透過扮演知名運動明星來進行遊戲。

Ex. NBA 2k

strategy 戰略

戰略型遊戲通常需要玩家具備做決策的能力,因為這將會在遊戲中扮演非常重要的關鍵。但其實很多時候,戰略遊戲也很靠運氣的。

Ex. 魔獸爭霸 III *Warcraft III*

racing 競速

主要以第一或第三人稱視角參與競速比賽,種類包含陸、海、空等各種車輛及飛行器的競賽。

Ex . 瑪利歐賽車 *Mario Kart*

12 {我只想一直睡下去}
To Sleep Is My True Calling

Rise and shine. 起床囉。

Rise and shine, you've slept for two days straight and it's Monday again.

起床囉，你睡了整整兩天，今天又是禮拜一囉。

sleepyhead (n.) 貪睡鬼

As a professional **sleepyhead**, I bring my pillow and blanket in my backpack for emergency naps.

身為職業級貪睡鬼，我會把枕頭跟被子用背包帶著，以免需要緊急午休。

pull an all-nighter (phr.) 熬夜

I used to be able to **pull all-nighters**, but now I can barely pull all-dayers.

以前我還能熬夜，現在我連白天都熬不下去了。

snore (v.) & (n.) 打呼；鼾聲

Crown **snores** every day. True story.

滴妹每天打呼。真心不騙。

 Hey, I've finished writing my new book! | 嘿！我的新書寫完囉！

 ... | ...

 Rise and shine! It's already 1 in the afternoon, **sleepyhead**! | 起床了啦！現在已經下午一點了，貪睡鬼！

 I can barely keep my eyes open. | 我忍不住睡意。

 Did you **pull an all-nighter** again? Time to get up! | 你昨晚又熬夜嗎？該起床了！

 ... | ...

 I filmed you **snoring**. I'm uploading it onto YouTube right now. | 我把你打呼的樣子錄起來了。我現在就要把它上傳到 YouTube 上。

 And I'm up! | 我起來了！

Extras

謝謝你看完這本書！今年阿滴英文團隊花了很多心力跟 EZ TALK 協力完成了這本書，在許多細節上都很要求，只為了帶給小滴最棒的內容。喜歡我們的教學的話，歡迎大家追蹤我們的各個社群平台，繼續學習生活中有趣的英文吧！

持續追蹤我們！

 滴妹 Crown

 crown_du

 滴妹

周邊商品
Fandora
 蝦皮購物

EZ TALK

跟著阿滴滴妹說出溜英文
網路人氣影片系列《10句常用英文》大補帖
附QR Code，音檔隨掃隨聽

作　　　者：阿滴&滴妹
協 作 者：邵培文
插　　　畫：A-Pei
責 任 編 輯：鄭莉璇
內 頁 設 計：蕭彥伶
內 頁 排 版：簡單瑛設
行 銷 企 劃　張爾芸

發 行 人：洪祺祥
副 總 經 理：洪偉傑
副 總 編 輯：曹仲堯
法 律 顧 問：建大法律事務所
財 務 顧 問：高威會計師事務所

出　　　版：日月文化出版股份有限公司
製　　　作：EZ叢書館
地　　　址：臺北市信義路三段151號8樓
電　　　話：(02) 2708-5509
傳　　　真：(02) 2708-6157
網　　　址：www.heliopolis.com.tw
郵 撥 帳 號：19716071日月文化出版股份有限公司

總 經 銷：聯合發行股份有限公司
電　　　話：(02) 2917-8022
傳　　　真：(02) 2915-7212

印　　　刷：中原造像股份有限公司
初　　　版：2018年7月
初版56刷：2024年4月
定　　　價：350元
I S B N：978-986-248-733-4

國家圖書館出版品預行編目 (CIP) 資料

跟著阿滴滴妹說出溜英文：網路人氣影片
系列 <<10 句常用英文>> 大補帖 / 阿滴
& 滴妹著 . -- 初版 . -- 臺北市：日月文化，
2018.07
　　面；　公分 . -- (EZ talk)
ISBN 978-986-248-733-4(平裝)
1. 英語 2. 會話
805.188　　　　　　　　　　107007933

《說出溜英文》全書音檔下載：http://bit.ly/eztalk_rdeng_new

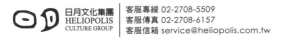

日月文化集團
HELIOPOLIS
CULTURE GROUP

客服專線 02-2708-5509
客服傳真 02-2708-6157
客服信箱 service@heliopolis.com.tw

日月文化集團 讀者服務部 收

10658 台北市信義路三段151號8樓

對折黏貼後，即可直接郵寄

日月文化網址：**www.heliopolis.com.tw**

最新消息、活動，請參考 FB 粉絲團

大量訂購，另有折扣優惠，請洽客服中心（詳見本頁上方所示連絡方式）。

日月文化 　　 EZ TALK 　　 EZ Japan 　　 EZ Korea

大好書屋・寶鼎出版・山岳文化・洪圖出版

日月文化集團
HELIOPOLIS
CULTURE GROUP

感謝您購買 跟著阿滴滴妹說出溜英文

為提供完整服務與快速資訊，請詳細填寫以下資料，傳真至02-2708-6157或免貼郵票寄回，我們將不定期提供您最新資訊及最新優惠。

1. 姓名：＿＿＿＿＿＿＿＿＿＿＿＿＿＿ 性別：□男　　□女

2. 生日：＿＿＿＿年＿＿＿＿月＿＿＿＿日 職業：＿＿＿＿＿＿

3. 電話：（請務必填寫一種聯絡方式）

　（日）＿＿＿＿＿＿＿＿＿（夜）＿＿＿＿＿＿＿＿＿（手機）＿＿＿＿＿＿＿＿＿

4. 地址：□□□＿＿＿＿＿＿＿＿＿＿＿＿＿＿＿＿＿＿＿＿＿＿

5. 電子信箱：＿＿＿＿＿＿＿＿＿＿＿＿＿＿＿＿＿＿＿＿＿

6. 您從何處購買此書？□＿＿＿＿＿＿＿縣/市＿＿＿＿＿＿＿書店/量販超商

　□＿＿＿＿＿＿＿網路書店　□書展　□郵購　□其他

7. 您何時購買此書？　　年　　月　　日

8. 您購買此書的原因：（可複選）
　□對書的主題有興趣　□作者　□出版社　□工作所需　□生活所需
　□資訊豐富　　□價格合理（若不合理，您覺得合理價格應為＿＿＿＿＿＿）
　□封面/版面編排　□其他＿＿＿＿＿＿＿＿＿＿＿＿＿＿＿

9. 您從何處得知這本書的消息：□書店　□網路／電子報　□量販超商　□報紙
　□雜誌　□廣播　□電視　□他人推薦　□其他

10. 您對本書的評價：（1.非常滿意 2.滿意 3.普通 4.不滿意 5.非常不滿意）
　書名＿＿＿＿　內容＿＿＿＿　封面設計＿＿＿＿　版面編排＿＿＿＿　文/譯筆＿＿＿＿

11. 您通常以何種方式購書？□書店　□網路　□傳真訂購　□郵政劃撥　□其他

12. 您最喜歡在何處買書？
　□＿＿＿＿＿＿＿縣/市＿＿＿＿＿＿＿書店/量販超商　□網路書店

13. 您希望我們未來出版何種主題的書？＿＿＿＿＿＿＿＿＿＿＿＿＿＿＿

14. 您認為本書還須改進的地方？提供我們的建議？

＿＿＿＿＿＿＿＿＿＿＿＿＿＿＿＿＿＿＿＿＿＿＿＿＿＿＿＿＿

＿＿＿＿＿＿＿＿＿＿＿＿＿＿＿＿＿＿＿＿＿＿＿＿＿＿＿＿＿

＿＿＿＿＿＿＿＿＿＿＿＿＿＿＿＿＿＿＿＿＿＿＿＿＿＿＿＿＿

＿＿＿＿＿＿＿＿＿＿＿＿＿＿＿＿＿＿＿＿＿＿＿＿＿＿＿＿＿